The
FOOLISH
HERO

The Journey to Create Your Destiny

SIMEN LOURDS SAMY

PARTRIDGE

To order additional copies of this book, contact
Toll Free +65 3165 7531 (Singapore)
Toll Free +60 3 3099 4412 (Malaysia)
orders.singapore@partridgepublishing.com

www.partridgepublishing.com/singapore

PROLOGUE

No sooner looms a daunting mountain than *faith* dissipates it like the morning dew in the sunlight.

His mother's advice, words to comfort and assure him, was shaping his thoughts. She was always reassuring, telling him that her prayers were constantly with him, that he had nothing to fear or worry about, and that he should realize that someone was watching over him. As it took shape, it formed itself into a reassurance: Be Not Afraid. He felt it spreading, a blue light, outward and downward filling his face, extending down his limbs, into the depths of his organs, consuming him with a newfound aura of confidence and belief that his life was about to change if he took the next steps. *Faith can shape a thought that can bring one to the abyss of change?* All he needed to do was act with conviction, and he would fly, not fall. They were rooting for him. "Go, Saman. Go on! You can do it now. Take that leap of *faith!*"

He awoke; still fettered by the vestiges of fear and doubt, he was kicking his legs out to free himself from the tangled blanket, but it was tightly wrapped around his ankles like iron shackles, imprisoning him. The blanket wrapped around his right ankle felt heavy; he had got his left untangled. He knew now where he was. *What was that about?* he thought to himself as he tried to make sense of it all. It was not new; he'd experienced it before—the dream.

It was darkest just before dawn. He was wading in the water. The cold crept up on him and threatened to immobilize him. He tried to keep the faith as he continued on until he reached the boat, which he clambered into. It took him with it as it slowly moved away from the safety of the bank where it had been tethered. When he could make things out through the clarity of the darkness his eyes had adjusted to, there was only water everywhere; and soon he caught sight of the moon that peeped from behind the dark cloud in the dark-blue water. He looked up and felt some relief. The boat continued past beyond where he had last dared venture and through the fog veil. He was gripped by a shroud of uncertainty but knew that he had to have faith if he desired to find what he sought. He had. Encouraged by it, the boat moved ever so slowly until it reached the edge where the water and the clouds joined. The sound had been getting progressively more audible. The roar was now deafening as his concentration was drawn away to it. He was not conscious of his earlier trepidation but of a new one.

"Go, Saman. Go. Have no fear. You can do it." They were hoping he'd take the next step.

If I fall, I will go down the abyss, a place from where there may be no return, he thought.

"If you fly, you'll soar!" They could not get through to him. They could only encourage, hope, and be there, watching over him. They could signal to him; he had to read the signs. He had to choose and dare.

Saman remembered the hurt he had experienced; he froze. His left foot caught in the blanket. He could not see through the cloud. He had ventured to the sound of the screaming water as it went into free fall down, echoing the silent groan of desperation and frustration deep in his bowels, and all he remembered was of its rippling echo throbbing in his mind. He moved between the dream and reality, wavering at the edge where the water joined the cloud. He had not made his choice—not yet. He dared not. Not yet, for he was reminded of it, again and again.

PART ONE

"**M**asing-masing keluarkan buku rampaian yang baru! Today we begin our first lesson in Malay. I know that you are all used to being instructed in English while you learn your grammar and vocabulary in Malay," her stern countenance conveyed in a language that he had understood and excelled in but which sounded foreign in *her* voice. "I want you to write your name, and get ready to learn the meaning of *buku rampaian*, which you ought to have worked out by now." Her quizzical look conveyed as she tossed back her short permed hair, curving itself just under her ears that made her face rounder, though it did not manage to soften the square jawline that mainly defined her face that fit the tone of her voice. "What are you waiting for?" a voice barked from behind.

He almost slid off the edge of the wooden chair that had its shellac worn off by the bottoms sliding onto and off it, perhaps since it was first placed there in Class 4 Red some ten or so years ago since the *New Straits Times* reported the story, curiously from Segamat. It was a small town, 111 kilometers away, about an hour and forty-nine minutes by car on the old

1

road. The small newspaper column announced on January 4, 1957, the construction of a new school that would cost the Johor state government $92,000. It was for boys in Kluang town. Saman wondered where the girls came from then. *Perhaps having the boys schooled with the girls will help the boys acquire the soft skills thought to be predominant among the female species?* he reasoned to himself. *On the other hand, perhaps it did not make economic sense.*

"Don't you have a new exercise book?" she snapped as his old one with just a few used pages was sent flying across the class, above his head and that of the others, and landed in the corridor outside the classroom.

He, too, snapped back from his reverie, muttering "So much for their soft skills" as he tried to catch himself before they spilled from his lips, but he was not in time. "What's that? I'm asking you about your *new exercise book*" was all he kept hearing as tears streamed down his embarrassed face, which searched around to see how many others were following his predicament.

"It's just twenty-five cents." Her head cocked back and down into her shoulders as four furrows appeared instantly on her forehead, which seemed to have the power to redden her face simultaneously. "If you can't afford that, why are you here? How do you hope to learn? You will come to nothing, I tell you!" *Just* hurt him more. He was a sensitive boy. With *just* that twenty-five cents, he could buy soda biscuits, which made six stacks of, more or less, six each that he and his three sisters and two brothers usually had for breakfast. The biscuits miraculously puffed up to double their size when left to soak in the black coffee, which completed their breakfast. They usually had a great time watching whose biscuit puffed up first, and the winner would get half a piece broken off from each of the others. Often the biscuit piece was less than half but never more. They were all unable to grasp fractions, it seemed. No one minded it, though, because the law of averages appeared to be working well as it, more or less, evened out if not on that day but certainly within the week.

"If you don't have your book tomorrow, you don't have to attend my class!" Now he felt about thirty-nine pairs of eyes trained on him. He was *hurt*, not because he did not have twenty-five cents but because he did. The money was for better use at home. "You will come to nothing!" bothered him as well, not because he believed it but because it seemed to define those who were poor, and he was poor, for now. The thought burned in his mind. He wanted to protest, but he wanted to learn, and such remonstrance might set him back more. She walked away. As she headed for the front of the classroom, she tossed back her hair; it again failed to soften the squareness of her jawline. As for Saman, he had a problem to solve by tomorrow.

———————— ⬥ ————————

But the recent yesteryears were unlike today. They were better times. He was sitting cradled in the red-and-blue checkered sarong that made a comfortable hammock that rocked slowly in a rhythmic fashion as his father shook his legs. He often did that when he was engrossed. So was Saman as he took in the intricacies of place values of numbers. If the last digit in the unit's place added up to more than nine, he learned to put a zero and carry one forward to the ten's place. It seemed to make sense as with the number ten. The ten's place value was to the left. So he figured that the same principle would apply between tens and hundreds. As he penciled in a zero and carried one forward to the next place, his dad ruffled his hair with his palm. Saman tilted his head to his left and upward to smile at his dad.

"Two hundred and forty-four and 416 make 660." He sought approval from his dad and got it from the ruffling of his hair. It was his favorite learning environment, and he seemed to pick things up fast.

On another occasion, he visited a sheep pen with his dad. His dad ran a mutton business in the wet market not far from home. He imported merino sheep from Australia that was shipped to Singapore and transported to Kluang by lorry. When they arrived, usually cramped in the open-top lorries that had to drive past his house, Saman always knew, as he could hear the bleating and would rush to the grilled windows through which he could see the sheep that looked big. Some had curved horns that made them intimidating. Fortunately, they were behind the grilles.

As soon as they were inside the sheep pen, Dad lifted Saman and set him amid the sheep. The wailing boy, terrified by the sight of hundreds of sheep in the sheep pen, stopped crying when he realized that they had backed off to a corner;

they were more afraid of him! His dad burst out laughing. Then he lifted Saman out and told him to watch as he opened the small gate that allowed the sheep to squeeze through one at a time to make their way out into the open grassy enclosure to run freely, much to their enthusiasm. Dad handed Saman a small branch that he had broken off from one of the hibiscus shrubs. The hibiscus shrubs grew close to the fence to conceal the enclosure from the view of any passersby. They also helped to soundproof the sheep enclosure from the noise of the passing cars and motorcycles coming from the road just outside so that the sheep would not be startled. When Saman held the stick across the gate about a foot and a half above the damp floor, the first sheep jumped over it to exit the pen. The next followed suit, and the third and fourth did the same.

"Now remove the stick," his dad commanded. To his delight, every sheep that reached the gate jumped over an imaginary stick before it made its way out. The sheep, too, learned by habit; unfortunately, they followed a herd mentality, Dad pointed out to him. Saman was puzzled, but the lesson stuck in his head. He realized that his dad had much to teach him and learning was fun.

Dad's mutton business was booming, and he employed a few helpers to shepherd the sheep. The workers cleaned the pen, gathered grass and bunches of leaves to feed them, and set them free daily within the enclosure to run around and get some fresh air and to exercise their muscles to enhance the quality of the meat. Dad was an enterprising man, and he also ran a canteen in the nearby British Army camp. Early mornings in the household was a beehive of activity as they brewed huge kettles of tea and coffee, fried noodles, and sliced bread to make sandwiches stuffed with egg and mayonnaise. Saman's grandfather had been a cook with the British Army during WWI in Africa. He made the mayonnaise from his special recipe. The air in the house was a potpourri of the aroma of freshly prepared snacks and specially brewed coffee. It woke Saman up every day, as he took in a whiff of the familiar smell.

After the war ended, Grandpa had returned to Malaya to set up his home and to raise a family. They had lived in Kluang since the early 1940s. Kluang was developing fast. All northbound and southbound trains on their way to and from Singapore stopped there.

Sometimes the sheep imported from Australia would be ferried to Kluang by train, arriving in the carriages of the goods train that usually arrived by noon. When the horn of the steam engine sounded, the children would head in the other direction to the grilled kitchen window, from which they could see the trains coming and going since the house was just fifteen to twenty meters from the railway tracks.

The older folks had become accustomed to telling time by the arrival and departure of the trains, and someone in the house would usually announce it. They had got so programmed by it that their body seemed to know intuitively when the afternoon mail train would arrive around three.

It was common for the trains to delay quite frequently. The cause for the delay became a topic of great debate in the household. Each interested adult offered his or her theory. It was another learning topic, as the children gained insights into train schedules, telling time, and understanding the economics of the town and the conditions that might disrupt it.

The owner of Jamaluddin Stores would pop by on occasion on his way to deliver the groceries on his large bicycle with a wooden box behind. He would not leave before lamenting the delay in his delivery schedule on account of the delay in the arrival of the goods train. Somehow that sometimes failed to settle the vehement disagreement as to the cause of the delay since the vindicated hypothesizer would be told by the other party that Jamaluddin could sometimes just be making excuses. There was never a day that passed without some lively banter or debate.

Before Saman started his schooling, Dad lost quite a bit of money through some bad investments and due to his overly trusting and helpful nature. If someone came to him in need, he did not say no. Saman had witnessed his dad ring the cash till and grab a handful of dollar notes without counting to hand over to the afflicted friend in need.

With the failing business, the laughter and joy faded a little at a time, and soon they had moved out into a rented house. Dad still had his mutton stall in the market, which he rented out for $210 a month. It was a decent amount.

He was a self-taught man who had a good command of the English language. He became a petition writer to make additional money to support the family. It was at this time that Saman started attending school, and the boy felt the impact of the changed circumstances. But Dad remained a trusting and kind man.

Once, a man arrived outside their house begging for money. He was with his wife and son, who was about ten years old like Saman. Dad told the man that he had no money to give him. But, if they wanted, they could have their lunch there. The hungry man and his family felt overjoyed and equally grateful. The eyes said as much.

Nowadays, meat was cooked only once a week on a Sunday in Saman's home. The children were excited in anticipation as the aroma from the kitchen wafted through the house.

The visiting family ate first; Saman and his younger siblings watched with disdain because there was not much food left after the visitors had eaten. As the grateful family of three left while continuing to thank Dad, the son's glance was on the shiny pair of boots sun-dried outside by Saman. It was his only pair of shoes, and he took great care to polish it with coconut oil so that it gleamed in the sun in preparation for church later in the evening.

Dad followed the little boy's gaze and asked him if he wanted the shoes. Dad asked Saman to hand the shoes to the boy, who was ever so grateful. That Sunday, Saman went to church in a pair of not-so-shiny canvas school shoes. It was in tatters, and Saman felt like a ragamuffin.

His dad said to Saman, "If you think our situation is bad, there are always others who are in greater need. If we can, we must help them. Someday, when we least expect it, someone else will be kind to us."

Years later, when he was on the verge of losing everything, he recalled that enlightening moment and his dad. It did not stop him from wondering how or why their circumstances had changed despite the kindness that his family, especially his dad and mom, displayed.

───────

Saman's father was a dashing young man, and he was an established businessman by the time he hit the midtwenties. Many lasses attracted him. Some wooed him, and with hormones raging, he had his fair share of the spoils. One such particular young lady was a close relative of his. Unfortunately, their union was frowned upon by the conservative community. With her advances spurned, her desire and the resultant unrequited love were so great that she cursed him in her heart when he chose someone else. The wedding with Saman's mother went on well. It was a grand wedding, and the merriment lasted a few days. The caterers were from the famous Jubilee Restaurant from across the causeway, summoned to prepare and serve their biryani, saffron rice that was pressure-cooked with the meat over a slow charcoal fire. There was music, singing, and dancing to entertain the guests.

The rejected young lady bore such hatred in her heart that she made a deal with the dark forces that the couple and their family would not live happily ever after. They would never come to anything! As it turned out, the wedding was held on May 4 and consummated before midnight, before May 5, St. George's Day. The couple, however, did not know the implication of this day.

Legend had it that May 4 was the eve of St. George's Day. "Do you not know that tonight, when the clock strikes midnight, all the evil things in the world will have full sway? As the new life of spring begins to emerge and the days become longer, the power of those who dwell in darkness begins to wane. With the blossoming of flowers and the sprouting of sweet basil, tomorrow—namely Saint George's Day—marks an end to their nefarious influence. So tonight, on its eve, vampires desperately rush to gather what power they can before the dawn comes," said the clairvoyant to the spurned young lady. "You must act now!"

The young lady had done her research. She had read that in Romania, where her clairvoyant friend came from, it was believed the living vampires or moroi gathered at the boundaries of towns at sunset. It was here they'd meet with strigoi, their dead counterparts, and strigele, living witches, to plan all the evil deeds they would carry out in the coming year. Before their influence would come to an end, the moroi must gather a year's worth of power on this night. They'd wander the boundaries seeking to prey on people and animals.

To gain power, moroi could steal the essence (mana) of creatures. This mana would be the quintessential talent of their prey. For instance, if the moroi would steal the power of a skunk, the skunk would no longer be able to release its foul odour. If his target was a person renowned for her skill in creating beautiful works of stained glass, she would no longer be able to create pieces of art. The moroi would either keep this power for themselves, offer it up to the strigoi they serve, or gift it to humans who had entered into terrible bargains with them.

Moroi also needed to take rain on this night. It was believed that when moroi washed themselves, the rain would fall. In times of drought, a nobleman would send all his men to wash because a moroi could easily be hidden among them. The moment the moroi's tail became wet, rain would pour from the heavens, and the drought would end.

Extra precautions must be taken to not fall victim to these prowling creatures on this unholy night. Windows should be anointed with garlic in the form of a cross. Indeed, every object in a home should have garlic on it. Special attention should be paid to doorways—especially their keyholes—and chimneys, for both are favorite entryways for vampires.

Valuable livestock or animals should also be rubbed down with garlic so that the moroi could not steal their mana. Millet could be scattered to ward off evil spirits, including vampires. To be safe, you should wear your shirt inside out and sleep with your head where your feet normally would be so the vampire would not be able to find you. If you were unsure the person calling you was a vampire, wait for them to call out your name three times, for a vampire could only call out twice. That was the legend or myth.

The spurned young lady cast a bewitching spell on Saman's father. However, it did not affect him or his young bride. Instead it skipped a generation and ricocheted onto his firstborn, Saman. Saman would bear the full brunt of the vile curse years hence.

———————

As he knelt and prayed, tears streamed down his face. Saman could not understand the inexplicable feeling within. He felt as if his heart was being grabbed and ripped out by some force from beyond. She was his first love. He had not spoken much to her all this while. He always greeted her with a beaming "Hi" each time he arranged to be close to her. She always returned it with a smile so sweet that he felt he could conquer any adversity or overcome any mountain that loomed before him. Such was the power it had. Such was the effect it had. She was fourteen; he was in the same class as her. She was his motivation. She was his muse as he composed poems. His first verse was so Keatsian:

Love is an inexplicable feeling
That rules in every being.

Lyn brought out the creativity in him, and he often daydreamed about their happy life together. In a couple of years, they had built their home sweet home, with a couple of kids running around merrily on the porch. They were so joyful, and it would last forever. It was just as the Fab Four had said.

Now she was leaving town with her mother and siblings. Her father had suddenly had a heart attack and died. Her mother decided to move to the capital about seventy-two miles away to make a living to feed the family. It was sudden, the decision to leave. They never got to say goodbye. What hurt was the fear that he would never see her again. He never did.

———————————————

The years rolled by, and he had got over the hurt, or so he thought. Saman was helping his neighbor Charles, the caretaker at the church, to put up the buntings in preparation for Christmas. Just then, he caught sight of her. She had short hair with soft curls. She was in a floral skirt and white blouse with puffed sleeves. "Can I cut a few of these flowers for the decorations inside?" He gazed into her innocent eyes. She smiled at him with an expectant look in her eyes. She leaned forward as she cut a few stalks of the African daisies that filled the circular cemented low wall built around the fountain at the main entrance. It was the first thing you saw as you entered the gates.

Saman knew her, and she, him. They sang in the choir together, and she was close to his younger siblings. They often mentioned that Jan did this or Jan did that. On one occasion, one of his siblings fell and scraped his knee. Jan attended to him and cleaned up the bruise before accompanying him back home. She did not spend much time there.

Whenever she dropped by Saman's house, she got on well with his widowed mother and sisters. They liked her. His sisters would tease him and encourage him to consider her. Now he did. He must speak with her at the dance on the feast day of St. Louis.

The local band played all their favorite tunes. Saman and his friends dressed in their best. He was wearing his favorite floral shirt, the only one he had. He saw that she was dancing with her friends and she was laughing. She was pretty. His friends knew of the crush he had on her. They also knew that Saman was mindful of his image. He was, after all, the youth head who guided all the younger boys in the church.

"Come on, ask her for a dance. Tell her how you feel. Don't lecture her, though. You're not her father." They all laughed out in unison. He finally plucked up enough courage, and after a glance toward the corner of the wooden house where his friends were sitting, he made his move.

The activity center was on the left as you entered through the gates. She was right in the center of the dance floor. He tapped the guy she was dancing with, and looking deep into her sparkling eyes, he said, "May I?" They were soon swaying to the tune. He tried to tell her something, but the music drowned his voice. She leaned toward him happily, and he said, "Don't you have your examination in a couple of months?" His righteous voice had got the better of him. They stopped dancing, and he never danced with her again.

As he returned to his friends, they burst out laughing for they knew what he might have done. "It's all right, bro. You have at least got over the first hurdle."

Jan was seventeen. She was sitting for the Malaysian Certificate of Education examination in November. Saman did not get to speak to her after that night although they saw each other every week in church.

One day, he heard that Jan was moving to Kuala Lumpur, the capital city of the country, 217 kilometers away. Jan's father had set up his new office there. There were more opportunities to be had there, and the whole family was uprooted from their home of nearly forty years by her father's decision. Saman was devastated. This time he did not cry, but he was hurt.

———————————◆———————————

Three years had passed. Saman was excited, yet he felt a dullness inside. He was going to meet Jan. She had written to him to say that she wanted to meet him. She was arriving in Kluang on December 5. He was eager to meet her. Had she changed? Did she harbor thoughts about him all this while? Why did it take three years? As he sat there on the bench on the platform of the railway station, he could not focus.

By this time, though, Saman had moved to Singapore and was enrolled in the teacher training college. He was happy that he had finally secured a decent job, and it paid well. He had enough money for himself, and he managed to send home RM400 (ringgit) a month to his mother.

With the RM210 that they got from the rental of the mutton stall that his dad had left behind, his mother had more than RM600 a month to see to the family expenses and to ensure that Saman's siblings got a proper education in school.

His two sisters after him were on their own. One worked in the Winitex Textile Factory that made high-quality fabric and handkerchiefs for export overseas. The other sister worked in a plywood factory producing plywood for furniture. Saman had worked in both before. They, too, brought home enough money to supplement the household income. Life was improving.

By this time, Saman had met someone he decided he would spend the rest of his life with. Jay was beautiful, shy, and spoke very little when others were around. He had told her he loved her. She brought happiness into his life. Jay was from a conservative family with three other siblings. They did not all approve of Saman for varying reasons. Jay was the third child in her family, and she had two older siblings and a younger one. Still, when they managed to be alone, they were happy.

Saman felt torn. Why was she coming back now? He was curious, yet he had made up his mind to tell Jan how his life made sense now, and it was partly due to Jay.

The train pulled into the station, and Jan peered out of the cabin. Jan smiled sweetly at Saman. Nothing seemed to have changed about her, but he had changed, or so he thought.

"Hi, Jan."

"Hi, Saman."

"Did you have a good trip? You look the same."

She laughed a little. "You have put on a little. Life must be treating you well?"

"You must be feeling hungry from that five-hour journey. Let's grab something to eat, shall we?" He did not wait for a reply as he took her arm and led her across the road. Immediately he was aware that he had acted instinctively. *Would she think I am taking advantage of her? Would I be giving her false hope?* His thoughts were disturbed. He knew what he was going to say to her.

"Shall we go to Savannah?" she quipped. It was a cozy coffeehouse about two blocks away smack in the busy part of the town. As soon as they got in there, they found a table close to the window overlooking the bright street below. She knew what to order, as she seemed to be familiar with the place. He did not miss that.

Saman got to the point. He pushed a letter that he and his friends back in Singapore had written. He had explained to them his predicament and his decision. He wanted to be clear and did not want to hurt Jan. He asked her, "In my place, would you leave Jay for Jan?"

The smile slowly left her. She looked down at her food. It seemed to last an eternity. Then she looked up and said, "Let's go. I've got a train to catch." Saman never saw her again.

———————————————

Jay and Saman saw each other a lot. They appeared to be a suitable couple to everyone who knew them.

Saman's mother was born in Singapore, while his dad was from Kluang. Saman's mother had left the city to settle in Kluang and had not returned to her birthplace for the next thirty-two years. She was a permanent resident of her new state, but she was stateless there. She could, however, return to the city to claim her right to citizenship, but she chose not to.

Saman's happiness was short-lived. Six years before he got married, he found out about Jay's secret. She had betrayed his trust. Saman felt humiliated that it was her paramour who informed him, and he had dared to invite Saman to their usual place of rendezvous to see for himself. He turned it down.

"Do you love her?"

"I've had women aged eighteen to forty-two," said the young man who had come to see Saman at his place of work. Jay's lover agreed to leave her, but he said, "I do not know if she can forget me."

That cut deeper. Saman loved Jay, and if truth be told, he felt desperate for her lover to vanish. He worked at the same place as Jay and had often given her a ride in his car. That was how the affair developed between them. Saman hoped to make the relationship he had with Jay work. It seemed to work out. They got married six years after that, but it was not without doubts, suspicions, and accusations. He could not get the betrayal out of his system.

Six years after they got married, he suspected that Jay was having an affair with her cousin. They had allowed him to stay with them, as he was much younger and had come to the city to look for a job. Everything seemed fine on the outside.

One day he noticed a hickey on her cousin's neck, and he asked Jay about it. She dismissed it, "How would I know? He hangs out late and probably has a girlfriend." Saman often worked late too and traveled overseas. He was not convinced but had let it pass.

By now, they had had a son born four years after they had married. Jay wanted another child. They had tried, but she had miscarriages along the way. It was during this time that she told Saman that she had consulted a gynecologist. He had informed her that if her husband's sperm count was low, they could try artificial insemination. Saman agreed and gave her a sample. It did not occur to him to accompany her to consult with the doctor. Everything seemed to happen so quickly as if he were under a spell. It occurred to him only years later that it could have been the reason.

That day, she surprised Saman when she returned home from the hospital. She told him that she was pregnant. There was no need for the sperm sample that Saman had given her. He was happy that they were going to have a second child. It did not occur to him to inquire how it had happened—the miracle.

When the baby was born, Jay behaved erratically at the ward. When Saman and her cousin visited her, they were shocked to find torn pieces of the newspaper strewn all over the floor. She was near hysterical, and she yelled at them. "Where did you go? Did you enjoy the coffee at the cafeteria?" Saman remained quiet. Then she turned to her cousin. "You too? Don't you have any responsibility?"

Now Saman felt queasy. "What does he have to do with any of this? Why should he feel responsible?" Twenty years later, he would recall these incidents. They would seem to add up. Again, he let it pass as postnatal blues. Her cousin comforted him as well as they left the hospital.

When the boy was reaching adulthood, Saman chanced upon text messages between Jay and her cousin. She alluded to the fact that the boy was just like him, hot-tempered but the first to show care. She also said that she was suffering and felt stuck. Her cousin had by then moved out and was happily married with a few kids of his own. But his response troubled Saman. He told Jay to pray and that God would show them a way out. "What way? A way out of what? Out of what?" Saman felt his head throb. Her cousin also said that he would be responsible and pay for the boy's education. Why?

Saman felt tortured. He confronted Jay, but she denied any wrongdoing. Saman tracked her, and he found that she had decided to delete all her conversations with her cousin. She was also very guarded about her phone. She changed the password and accused Saman of checking her phone without her knowledge. It was true. He had done that, but he had had a strange prompting to do so. He had never done that in all their thirty years together. It was on the death anniversary of his father that something told him to do that, and he chanced upon her secret.

Saman finally realized that although he could not be sure, his suspicions from twenty years back could not be unfounded. Yet he loved the boy dearly, and the boy loved him too. He made up his mind that for the sake of his son, he would not go further by taking action against Jay. He also realized that he had made the mistake of giving her another opportunity when he had first discovered that she had betrayed his trust with her first lover.

Saman learned the lesson to forgive but not to forget. He wondered if he had made the wrong choice. He could not be sure; one could not be sure that the road not traveled would be the right one. But the road he chose was not the one.

Saman advised his sons that if their girlfriend or fiancée betrayed their trust, they should not give her another chance. He was not unforgiving. He did not want his children to go through the same mental anguish that he had experienced for thirty years and that he was still experiencing every day. It was a father's love.

The hurt remained, and so did the curse cast on May 4, 1957, unknown to Saman.

The phone rang at Saman's workplace. He was expecting it, so he sat at the table nearest the telephone in the staffroom. To conceal his excitement from the others who by now had become accustomed to the incoming calls at this time every other day, he busied himself with grading his student's homework. He picked up the telephone call as the other staff exchanged giggles. They had been enjoying his conversation with her.

"Hi, have you had your lunch?" she tried to sound matter-of-fact.

"The other day at your cousin's place felt good."

"But how about Jay?"

"Look, Maria. Do you like me?"

"When I think about you and Jay, I ..." He could detect the tension in her voice.

Maria was Jay's neighbor, and they had been so for almost twenty years. Jay was a little older, and Maria looked up to her. They had enjoyed a sisterly relationship up until then. She was often at Jay's place when Saman dropped by, and they had got acquainted. Saman, like Jay, helped Maria with her schoolwork. Jay used to help Maria when she was younger, but when she moved to high school, Saman took over. They spent a lot of time together since the work was demanding. Jay did not mind.

Saman realized that Maria was getting too close for comfort. He had, on occasion, caught her staring at him. When his eyes locked with hers, she did not look away. She sat close to him when she wanted him to help her with her assignments. Saman sensed the urge in him, and he could not resist; he did not resist it.

It was their secret. Nobody else in the house noticed it. Jay did not seem aware of it either. Perhaps she had other interests in her mind to take notice of anything strange about Maria's growing closeness to Saman.

They were all invited to the house of Maria's cousin for a housewarming party. Jay's family had known Maria's cousin well too. After dinner, everybody sat down for a game of cards as was a common practice among them. They wagered inconsequential bets, as the focus was not to try to win but to enjoy one another's camaraderie and to catch up on the latest gossip.

Maria sat next to Saman. Her excuse was that she was not familiar with the game of blackjack and was hoping that Saman would guide her. Soon, Saman realized that Maria was playing footsy with him. He withdrew his foot, but she persisted. Saman stole a sideways glance, and she looked at him as if nothing was amiss. He then felt a hand on his thigh under the overhanging tablecloth. Saman hurriedly surveyed the others. They were conscientiously studying the cards in their hands. He let her continue.

They continued their rendezvous every time Saman was over at Jay's place. Some days, Jay would ask if Saman could come over earlier because Maria had a problem with her assignment; she needed help with it urgently. Saman obliged her willingly. Each time, their attraction to the other grew.

"I have to see you," he said. "We can talk about this then."

Maria was quiet.

———————◆———————

Saman waited at the Cathay Cinema. He took her arm and walked across the road to the Rendezvous Restaurant that sat at the junction between Selegie Road and Bras Basah Road. It was a popular eatery famous for its *nasi padang*, an Indonesian rice dish topped with different curried meat or seafood and vegetables of one's choice. He did not think anyone they knew would be there.

"What if someone sees us?"

"We are not doing anything wrong. We are just enjoying a drink together," Saman reasoned. Maria looked down. "Look, Maria. We can't go on like this. I can't go on like this. I need to know."

"I can't betray Jay. You know that."

"I don't feel the same way with Jay as I do with you."

"But you are engaged to Jay."

"I know that. I need to know from you how you feel about us."

She sensed the agitation in his voice. She knew he wanted her to commit, but she wanted him to arrange everything. Should he not tell Jay first? Not about them but that he did not love her? Deep down, they wanted to be with each other more than anything else. They were hoping desperately for the other to make the first move. Neither of them did.

<hr />

Maria was the bridesmaid at the wedding. Saman's best friend drove the wedding car, while his brother was the best man. After the ceremony in the church, they made their way to Saman's house for the customary rituals that followed the Indian traditions. Saman sat next to Jay in the back seat. Maria sat on his left. The driver quipped that Saman was the luckiest groom in the world as he had one sister on his right and *one* on his left. Saman's brother and his new wife broke into laughter. Saman and Maria remained quiet. He felt the warmth of her bridesmaid's gown against his leg.

The painful love affair between Saman and Maria continued for the next twenty years. Maria had married someone. They seemed happy and had two children of their own. They had all become as close as family. Each Christmas, they would make it a point to spend one day at each other's home.

The children loved the gatherings, and so did Jay and Maria's husband. Saman cherished the opportunity to see Maria, and he hoped she felt the same way too. When she served drinks or passed the delicacies around, her fingers would always graze Saman's. She would gently step on his toes as she offered him a piece of the suji cake. "I know you are waiting for this, aren't you?" she would say, looking deep into his eyes. It was that same look that she had twenty years ago when she first sat with her thigh against his and she intently listened to his explanation of the meaning of Coleridge's poem "Love":

> You mould my Hopes, you fashion me within;
> And to the leading Love-throb in the Heart
> Thro' all my Being, thro' my pulses beat;
> You lie in all my many Thoughts, like Light,
> Like the fair light of Dawn, or summer Eve
> On rippling Stream, or cloud-reflecting Lake.
> And looking to the Heaven, that bends above you,
> How oft! I bless the Lot, that made me love you.

Saman and Maria were not happily married. They held on to their secret and the memories.

———————————

As he wandered through the wilderness, Saman was overcome with confusion—confusion about his life. No, it was not only in love that he had lost. His professional life was troubling him as well. On the surface, he appeared to be progressing well. He started teaching in an elementary school after graduating from the teachers college he was in. He graduated two years after he had seen Jan leave from the Kluang railway station.

Things stabilized somewhat, and then he met the stranger who narrated to him Jay's secret. Every time he seemed to be riding a wave. And then before he knew it, he was down on a trough. The years between 1982 and 1988 was also the period of great excitement in his life. That was when he discovered Maria. She was like an antidote that helped to dull the pain. She was also the breath of fresh air he needed to avoid being suffocated by life. Maria encouraged Saman to improve himself, and he did. He won a scholarship to the local university. He had to first pass the General Certificate Advanced level examination first. Focusing on it afforded him the distraction from his troubles.

Saman majored in English literature at the university. Saman felt he was unlike the protagonist in Christopher Marlowe's *Doctor Faustus*. Faustus despaired when he had the opportunity to turn his life around by choosing hope through divine forgiveness. Saman persevered. He journeyed through life and rose to be a head teacher.

The size and quality of his abode changed with the times. He sold his first apartment and bought a private condominium. He drove a Mercedes Benz, trying to keep up with the Joneses. Yet Saman realized that there was a constant void in his life. The wistfulness remained. He tried to camouflage it with the trappings of materialism, but it remained.

Often at night, he lay awake in bed. He dreamed of and yearned for that which he missed dearly. He tried to seek it in the investments he made in the stock market. He lost a fortune because that was not it.

Saman's thoughts vacillated between suspicion and faith. He could not shake off the betrayal by his wife. At the same time, the guilt of his secret love for Maria consumed him. He kept thinking about his inability to make the right choice.

Was he different from Faustus? By not having the courage to choose Maria, had he not despaired? Did his class one honors in English amount to anything if he was not able to apply the lesson that he imbibed from Marlowe?

Saman recalled the advice given by the Oracle as he voraciously read everything he could get hold of before he invested his money. What was the point of being able to forecast the next crisis if you had not prepared yourself to take action to avoid the calamity? It was not enough to merely know something—anything. Saman realized that he had not acted when it mattered.

He was in a daze. All of a sudden, without warning, Saman saw Alice in Wonderland at the forked road. He remembered what the Cheshire cat said to Alice: "It does not matter what road you take if you do not know where you are going." Did he know where he was going? Did he know what he wanted?

Yet he wanted peace in the household. He wanted happiness for his extended family. He did not want to cause chaos. He was, after all, seen as the leader. He was the leader among his siblings, and he was the leader among his friends, who always consulted him when in doubt. He had tried to set the example. That was also something that he had wanted. He wanted to progress along that path, to be respected and admired. If he was unhappy, then did it mean it was not the road he desired?

The thoughts inundated him. *What should I do?*

"Pray. Ask, and you shall receive, my dear friend." Saman turned around, and it was Appu, his old friend. He thought he recognized that familiar voice.

"What are you doing here?"

"It's my hometown. I should be asking you that question. I was driving by, and I thought I spotted your car in the church car park. When did you get back?"

"Yesterday. It's been three years—a long time."

"Too long."

"You see, I—"

Appu held up his palm to Saman and cut him off before he could say anymore. "You don't need to explain anything. We have our ups and downs, but it's good to see you, Saman."

Saman nodded his acknowledgment. They had been childhood friends and neighbors for time immemorial. They went to school together, stole rambutans from the neighborhood together, only to satisfy their hungry stomach. They knew everything about each other, almost.

"Something's bothering you. You are not the Saman I know."

"What do you mean? I'm always the same."

"No, you are not. I can tell from the way you respond. You are always optimistic, full of life, our thought leader."

Saman looked at his friend with affection. He missed him; he missed their friendship.

"I'm going to be home, Saman. If you need to talk, you know where to find me. I will leave you both with your thoughts." He gestured with his head toward a grotto that housed the infant Jesus that was next to his car. Saman stared blankly at Appu's disappearing back. He still had the same gait, all five foot ten inches of him.

Saman remembered how they scrounged around to find a few coins to buy *roti prata* from the stall just behind their houses, next to the Mariamman Temple along the road leading to the army camp, and shared it. After that, they had made their way to the small shed that stored the railcar a stone's throw from there to share a smoke. It was the life of a teenager, a simple but satisfying one. Saman caught himself smiling as he reminisced about their youth. It had been months since he last recalled smiling. There was something about one's hometown that did this. The familiar surroundings, the faces one trusted, and the scents and the air combined to give assurance that all was well.

Saman turned to look at the grotto as he connected through his thoughts what was weighing on his mind. When his son was born, the chief pediatrician had broken the shocking news to him.

"Your boy has a hole in his heart."

"What?"

"Look, it's my job to tell it as it is. It may close in a month, a year, or even after his teenage years."

"Doctor, can I get a second opinion? I hope you don't—"

"Well, I have more than seventeen years of experience, and I have never been wrong."

"I understand, but he is my firstborn."

"My colleague from the UK is on attachment here from next week. If you like, I can arrange for him to speak with you after he has reviewed your son's case."

"Thank you, doctor."

"See you at two in the afternoon next Wednesday."

Without looking back, he walked out of the room. When Saman returned to the ward, he looked at Jay. She was still in a daze from the eight-hour labor. His boy was asleep in his cot next to his mother.

Saman decided to return to the familiar surrounding where he felt comforted. He was back in Kluang, his hometown. As he gazed at the grotto, he remembered his catechism class under the coniferous tree with Sister Elvira.

"Say the infant Jesus prayer when you are troubled," she said, and she taught the children gathered around her how to say the prayer.

The following Wednesday, he was punctual for his appointment with the doctor. He saw the shiny patch at the back of the head of a man in his white coat. When he turned around, he recognized Dr. Samuel, his son's pediatrician, but not the other Caucasian man. He assumed it must be the visiting specialist.

As they walked toward him, Saman's heart started beating faster. He could hear it.

"We have some news for you."

"Doctor, please. Is there anything you can do?"

"Nothing, but there's no need for that. Your boy is fine. The murmur I heard earlier was due to the fluid in his lungs. His heart is fine. I must admit that I am surprised myself. I must be getting old." He turned to look at the Caucasian man before he could complete his sentence.

Tears welled up in his eyes. Saman could not remember if he thanked the two men as he hurriedly left to see Jay and his son. He had not told Jay anything about the doctor's earlier diagnosis. Now he did not feel the need to say anything to her either.

Saman had witnessed the power of faith. The sincerity with which he appealed to the divine power and the focus of his thoughts helped to move what seemed an immovable mountain. It was not the first time that he had experienced a miracle.

Saman and Jay had to attend a marriage preparatory course as required by their faith before they officially tied the knot. A doctor and his wife, a couple with many years of experience in married life, conducted the course. There were other couples there. They learned the importance of the spirit of forgiveness and tolerance to make a marriage work well. The doctor and his wife also emphasized the importance of

God-centered family life. Both Saman and Jay were born and baptized Christians. Saman, in particular, spent most of his younger days in activities in the church in his hometown.

After the fortnightly course ended, they came to hear about an apparition of the Blessed Mother in Medjugorje. Curious to learn more about it, Saman subscribed to receive a monthly newsletter from the Marian Centre that disseminated updates on the developments in Medjugorje. In one of the monthly news, Saman read about the request to pray for sinners and their conversion. The newsletter invited devotees to read the Gospel passage Matthew 6:24–34 daily. Thinking that there was no harm in praying for others, Saman faithfully followed this practice since June 1988 when he had first read the invitation in the newsletter.

Saman was not a religious person, but he was God-fearing. It was ingrained in him by his mother from a young age. Saman did not think much of it and just incorporated it into his daily morning prayers before he set out. He was then in the university. Soon, four years passed. One of the papers that Saman sat for in his final examinations was in the history of English. It was a little more demanding than the other examination papers since students had to transcribe texts written in Old English, such as those dating back to AD 700 like *Beowulf*.

English is a Germanic language with influences from many other languages because of trade links with other nations and as a result of conquests of territories. The languages spoken in these territories were different from Old English itself, hence the strange words.

Most of the students dreaded the paper. When the day for the examination arrived, Saman said the usual morning prayers and headed to the Temasek Hall, the venue of the final examinations.

"You may turn over the question paper now. Please read the instructions carefully. You may begin now," the voice of the invigilator blared from the loudspeakers on the side of the hall.

Saman had done well in all the other papers. He knew it, and if he did well on this paper, he could end up top of his class. He felt nervous but also quietly confident.

The questions were difficult; he expected that. Saman looked up from the paper to survey the hall. He saw a sea of heads. He returned to the question and tried to figure out the words. He had two hours and a half to do so. Then something caught his eye. He recognized a few words: *God, possession.* Where had he seen them before? Then as if in a flash, he realized that it came from an Old English text taken from the Gospel of Matthew 6:24–34. He knew it by heart! He felt goose bumps on his hands, and he was excited.

Without much effort, he wrote out the entire passage from memory. He had etched the words in his mind, although he had been mouthing them without giving much thought. But he had done it faithfully every day.

Before the others raised their bowed heads, Saman had completed his final paper. He felt confident in himself. He was pleased that he had managed to complete the entire examination without too much difficulty.

That day, Saman first realized the power of faith. It dawned on him that if he practiced something until it became automatic, he would be able to acquire a new skill or learn something through deep understanding.

————————

From the time he was an acolyte in church, Saman had had a strong faith in God. He lived less than a 150 feet from the church. The children spent a lot of time there. On Saturdays, they all attended catechism classes taken by the Canossian nuns. After that, they would adjourn for mass. On weekdays, Saman and his good friend Ted Nathan took turns to be acolytes for the daily morning service before they headed off to school.

Saman and his friends were also actively engaged in youth activities. They were part of the Legion of Mary, they sang in the choir, and they helped out by cleaning the church grounds and even mowing the grass in the cemetery just behind the church. For their efforts, they received twenty ringgit per month for every grave that they helped to upkeep. The money went into the youth coffers, and it helped to fund their trips to the seaside at Mersing or in Malacca. They were quite an enterprising group of boys. More importantly, these activities kept them engaged and away from the street corner gangs that were a growing menace among youth.

Once he moved away from his hometown, things began to change. It was common when someone moved away from the control center of his life. Sitting by the fountain, Saman noticed that every time he dropped a pebble into the water, ripples fanned out from the center. They were more pronounced and had firmer lines closer to the center. It left an indelible mark on him, although he did not realize then that his life would not be any different if he did not stay close to the values that formed his center of control.

As Saman progressed in his professional life, he was busier with work. He had greater responsibility for the welfare of his staff, and he handled more projects. Saman felt respected.

Often his work required him to work on weekends to meet tight deadlines. Saman grew more attached to his work, and he paid less attention to his internal growth. Mentally he was growing as he read more and quite diversely. Spiritually he was regressing. He did not notice the change, though. His center was shifting.

The miracles he had experienced in his time of need had failed to make a lasting impression on him, it seemed. When previously he turned to his faith to guide him and inspire him, now he turned to other gurus. Saman was not completely satisfied with his job. It did not meet his expectations of being constantly challenged, and he craved a new challenge.

It was at this time that the financial crisis of 2000 brought about a stock market crash. Soon the devastation of the World Trade Center in New York on September 11 shook the world. Terrorism was on the rise. Singapore felt its effects too. Mas

Selamat, a confessed extremist, escaped from the Whitley Road Detention Centre. He was held captive there by the authorities. There was a round-the-clock search for him. Saman had to return in the middle of the night to his school. Selected personnel searched the science laboratories. They made sure to lock away corrosive chemicals. The authorities displayed photographs of the fugitive all over the tiny island to alert residents to be wary of him. They reminded the people to report him to the police if they spotted him anywhere. The threat posed by such militants was real, and it was a time gripped by the uncertainty that came with fear.

The same fear generated a negative energy that pervaded Saman's mind. He wanted to safeguard the future of his family, especially that of his children. His thoughts drifted in different directions.

"How can I grow my wealth for the sake of my children?" As he delved more into the world of wealth and investments, he read widely and distilled many lessons from the financial gurus. Many of these lessons were invaluable; some others grew out of greed.

New to this game, Saman lost a lot of his savings. Greed drove him to think of outsmarting the next guy. When he learned about binary options that promised higher returns than the stock market, he plumped for it. Many of these companies had registered in the Cayman Islands or Cyprus. They were able to avoid the rules and corporate governance of the traditional financial centers in the world. Saman was gullible enough to trust them.

"Ling, be careful. I see you taking so many foreign calls. Who are these people?" Jay tried to warn him. She called him *Ling*, short for darling.

Saman paid little notice. "I know what I'm doing," he would retort. His distrust in her partly made him ignore her well-intentioned advice. He was to realize the importance of the right life partner who'd help a man be successful in life. One day he read that Warren Buffet, Bill Gates, and others like them attributed their success in life to a good spouse, someone who supported them and who loved them.

By now, Saman was on the verge of debt, and he was falling behind in his monthly payments. His mortgage was outstanding, as were the other bills. Saman turned first to licensed moneylenders and then to the unlicensed ones to make ends meet. When he was not able to service their interest payments, they harassed him and threatened to harm his family.

The 2008 global financial crisis saw many businesses go belly-up. Saman knew that if he had cash, he could buy up many stocks whose price had plummeted, as speculators and investors took refuge from the market turmoil.

Each time an opportunity arose, he was not ready to take advantage. It was due, in part, to his ill-timed and ill-advised forays into the market, pinning his hopes on unknown investment products.

Saman found himself in a bind. On one occasion, he was to meet a moneylender to collect the loan promised to him. He walked up to an apartment and knocked on the door. Realizing that he was not in the right place, he tried to leave.

When he walked out of the elevator, three policemen arrested him. The family that lived in the apartment thought that he was one of the moneylender's runners who came there to harass them as they had done before. Saman walked straight into a trap set for him by a dishonest moneylender.

Saman spent the night in a lockup. He had never seen the inside of one, but now he did. Fortunately for him, the police realized that he was a victim of a scam and released him on bail. Saman had to report to the police station once a month as part of his bail orders.

As his debts mounted, his troubles worsened. His creditors were coming after him, as he had fallen behind in his payments. Before long, his creditors demanded payment through the courts. They declared that he had to pay up the money he owed, the sum of $38,000 outstanding on his credit card. Saman had been making prompt payments since he owned the credit card in 2005. In 2009, the issuing bank stopped his access to the credit card, but they kept charging him the full effective rate of the interest as if he was using the card. All the time, he continued making the minimum payments. In 2018, he had fallen behind in payments by several months. Still they charged him the full amount that they initially disbursed to him in the card.

His house mortgage was now in trouble. His bank wanted him to pay $42,000 or face eviction. His monthly mortgage was $2,090. Saman appealed for help and managed to raise $24,000 in May 2019. He was evicted from his home of twenty years by court order on May 28, 2019.

Saman spent the next two years in spiritual limbo. On December 30, 2019, the world heard about the COVID-19 virus. By April of the following year, most countries were in lockdown. People could not travel, businesses were not open, and supermarkets rationed how much each customer could buy essential goods. People started working from home, as it was dangerous to come into contact with one another. The government of each country introduced social distancing measures. As the economy came to a standstill, many businesses folded.

Saman sought some consolation in the fact that he was affected by the pandemic like the others. He was not. His predicament was a result of his carelessness with his money and because of his overly trusting nature.

Saman's life had taken a nosedive into the abyss. He had made the wrong choices, and he had failed to heed the warning signs and signals sent to him. When he reread Aesop's advice given in 600 BC, it struck him like a bolt of thunder: "A bird in the hand is worth two in the bush."

"The best theories are the ones that are simple and intuitive," Saman tried to convince his friends. They were writing their final-year theses. He had lectured the same advice to his colleagues during training sessions. "Do not overcomplicate. Try to keep it simple." Yet he had missed the most basic of advice. Saman recalled the scene from *The Godfather* movie when Michael Corleone addressed his recalcitrant older brother, "It's not easy to be a son, Fredo."

It is easy to tell people what to do; it is not easy to follow the same advice. A good son follows what his father taught him.

"Do what is right," said the general. General Norman's voice reverberated through the packed hall. It was at the National Achievers Congress, an annual event that brought some of the captains of industry and thought leaders together to deliver their message of inspiration to the young and eager learners. Saman was one of them, just starting in the workforce. He was thrilled to be there among thousands of others.

General Norman, who had fought in the Gulf War, was narrating his experience when he was at the Pentagon as a young military attaché to one of the generals. One day, the general was leaving for an important meeting, and he was briefing the young Norman, who was a nervous wreck. He felt helpless without the general around and was afraid that he could not handle the responsibility.

"What if—" he started, but the general stopped him midsentence. Norman was trying to commit to memory as much of the SOPs he needed as it was possible. That way he just had to follow the rule book should something crop up.

"When you are in charge, take command! And do what is right." Then he marched off to board the waiting helicopter, leaving the young attaché looking at the back of the wise general.

Saman scribbled the general's orders in his notebook: Do what is right!

He also scribbled "How will I know that it is right?" in the margin. Many years later, he would find out.

———————

Many things were running through his mind as Saman sat at his desk. "What had happened to me in the years between my graduation from university and the present?" he wondered aloud. "I have read so much. I've heard from so many experts telling me how to be successful in life. Life has taught me many invaluable lessons as well. Have I not tried to follow some of them? Then why am I in this situation?"

"You know what to do," a voice from within told him. Saman was startled, as his train of thought was interrupted. He looked around the room. He was alone.

"I do? I do." He felt he had to go away from all this, his present situation. He needed to silence the voice that was telling him that there was no way out. He had to look deep within himself. Yes, he recalled, "Those who look outside are dreaming; those who look within awaken."

"Who was it who said that?" He knew, but it did not register just now. Saman decided that he needed to put first things first and find solace in the quiet away from it all for a while. He must unclutter the clutter in his mind. But where will he go?

———————

It was Carl Jung who said that! Yes! Now he recalled: "Those who look outside are dreaming; those who look within awaken." Others followed after him. Sadhguru, a mystic from India, had been traveling the world selling his idea of inner engineering as he called it. It was similar, like old wine in new bottles, but they all meant well, and they meant the same thing.

Saman was beginning to make connections between these ideas. Stock phrases floated in his mind: "The magic is within." "Seek, and you will find." "Do not be afraid to give up the good to go for the great."

Saman himself had always believed in looking inward for answers. He trusted his gut. His theory was similar: Man needs to expose himself to as many different ideas and things as possible. The subconscious mind stores them. They are disconnected. When you need answers to problems and you focus on finding a solution, the brain can make the connections between these disparate things to offer a solution. That is the *aha!* moment, no different to the exhilaration experienced by Archimedes, Mozart, Newton, or Einstein. Saman had often shared his theory with his friends and staff who cared to listen. He knew it intuitively.

Now as he read and listened to the ideas of others, they fit in. These ideas remained just that. He could only realize them if he did one thing, just one—act! He related to Napoleon Hill's belief that it appears to be that the subconscious mind is the only doorway to approach infinite intelligence. A man has absolute control over only one thing—his thoughts. If he uses his thoughts to find a way to connect with the universal intelligence, he can create or achieve anything.

"That universal intelligence is God to some. It can be what we refer to as nature. It is the celestial beings of the universe to others. Or it is the light, the force, the power to still others," Saman surmised.

Saman concluded that he had to have faith and confidence. Then he needed a crystal-clear goal. With focus and perseverance, regardless of what other people might think or say, he had to bear that thought in his mind. It did not matter if he did not know how he would get there. He could change his plan as he acted on it. But he had to take action and not be distracted. With this singularity of purpose and focus, what he'd do would guide him on his path toward his goal.

Just then, he remembered the morning sermon. He followed the daily mass online because the pandemic restricted physical attendance at church. "Follow me!" it said. Saman knew he had to follow that thought he had.

———

Saman was alone with his thoughts. He was sitting at the confluence of the two rivers. Klang River flows through Kuala Lumpur, the capital of Malaysia, eventually flowing into the Strait of Malacca. It would have traveled a distance of 120 kilometers to do so. One of its eleven tributaries is the Gombak River. Where it meets the Klang River is the origin of Kuala Lumpur's name, which translates into "the muddy basin."

It was here that Saman traveled back to in search of answers. Saman's dad was born in Klang. As Saman sat on the banks of Klang River, looking out as far as his eyes could see, he felt a serenity he had never experienced before. *Perhaps going back to one's roots can do that*, he thought to himself; he was not sure. As the gentle breeze that was blowing caressed his face, battered by years of facing the headwind, his eyes narrowed. They focused intently on a point in the river. It was a darker color than the waters that flowed toward it. Saman realized that it was the point at which the two rivers met. He looked at his watch. It was eleven past eleven. He raised his head again to focus on where he was just before now.

Saman realized that the different roads he had taken as he journeyed through life meant the same thing. The confluence of the rivers was narrower than its mouth before it opened out into the sea. It dawned on him that if he understood how everything came together, then it would open out to the other side, what he was seeking. The river had to go through this narrow point before it entered the vast sea. It started making sense to him, but he had to concentrate hard to fathom how it all came together to help him move forward. He still did not know what he should do next and how he ought to go about it, but he was calm.

"The two rivers balance each other," he said softly to himself. "How do they do that?" he asked himself. "Klang … Klang is where dad was born. How did I come to be?" Saman looked at the same point where the two rivers joined each other. It was the closest they had been, and then they brought forth, as it were, the one river that was much wider at the river mouth.

"Think! Concentrate!" he commanded himself.

As the sun descended in the sky toward his right, it was starting to set.

"Dad and mom and then me," he said aloud. A smile broke out from the sides of his mouth. "Yes!" Saman realized that he had the qualities of both his parents, yet he had always tried to be more like his dad—strong on the outside, determined, outspoken, and brave. He had not given much emphasis to the qualities he had inherited from his mom. She was quieter, observant, humble, and hardworking; yet in all this, she displayed a stoicism that had brought him to this point after his dad died prematurely.

Saman knew that it was going to be tough working on these qualities. He had to look within; it was by doing so that he had come to know what he now did. Saman was not balanced. The masculinity in him needed the femininity to make him a better person, like Leonardo da Vinci's *Vitruvian Man*, in perfect proportion and symmetry.

Saman also knew that knowing this meant nothing. He had to become it. That required hard work, focus, patience, a desire, and the firm belief that he would get there. First, he had to visualize himself as the new person, the new Saman. Who did he want to become?

PART TWO

"What are you looking for?"

"I left it here, but now it's gone."

"Unless you tell me what it is, how can I help you?"

Saman turned his head from the coffee table to Jay. He did not say anything to her.

Jay shook her head, shrugged her shoulders, and left the living room. Saman continued to rummage through the books that he had left on the table. Saman always had a few books on the coffee table. He read them at the same time; he read a few pages of one book and then switched to another. He would come back to the first book when he felt the need. He liked them to be left there and not moved about as Jay often did. She was always rearranging his things. He was annoyed with himself for letting her.

Saman's frustration was growing by the minute. He felt that way when he could not find something where he had last placed it. Impatience was his biggest weakness.

Saman could hear his wife mumbling something about his carelessness. He tried not to pay attention to it, but he did.

"Are they resting on your forehead?" she called out from the bedroom.

Saman's hand instinctively reached out to his forehead; it was there—his glasses. He removed it and looked at it sheepishly, occasionally glancing in the direction of the bedroom.

"I suppose you found it where you had last left it?"

He knew that he had them on when he was last reading "Ulysses" by Lord Alfred Tennyson. The collection of poems was on the table, so his glasses should be there. But how did she know he was looking for them?

He could not blame Jay this time, for she could not have rearranged his things as he often suspected her of doing. She certainly could not have placed them on his forehead. He smiled to himself.

Just then, Jay walked out of the bedroom. Seeing him with the glasses in his hand, she shook her head again and smiled.

Saman thought to himself, *From now on, I should first search myself.*

"Sing us a song," they said. The family gathered for the usual Christmas lunch. After a sumptuous meal comprising the entire range of meat varieties and fish, complemented by a spread of salads, Saman and his family usually broke into two groups; one played a game of cards, the other adjourned to singing to make merry and to round off the celebrations.

"Let's begin with a Christmas carol," Saman suggested, and he proceeded to belt out his favorite in his soprano voice. It cracked a little in some parts, which he and the others, who had become accustomed to his flawless renditions, attributed to the food and free flow of wine and spirits. They were not wanting.

As the merriment started winding down, someone in the group thought aloud, "I notice you are wearing that stone. What's with it?"

"Yes, I have noticed it too," said another, "and on the index finger, which is unusual."

Saman smiled but did not say anything. He was determined not to speak much. Saman was practicing holding back when he felt the urge to speak, which did not need encouragement from anyone. He was naturally effusive and bold. He did not shy from expressing his views. It was not easy, as he itched to tell them. But he continued to smile.

"It's a yellow sapphire," another one among those gathered there said. Yellow sapphire stones were among the most valued of the Vedic stones.

"I read somewhere that the yellow sapphire has links to Jupiter, guru, or the teacher."

"It must enhance his voice," someone joked, and everyone burst out laughing. They were all in high spirits.

Saman felt pleased. He had succeeded in one of his attempts, although he needed to practice being more patient more consistently. It suddenly occurred to him that without saying much, he had allowed the others to express themselves and discover what they were curious about by themselves. He just had to be there; less was more. As he quietly smiled to himself, Saman recalled the Buddha's teaching about the power of smiling and remaining silent: "A smile is *a way* to solve problems, and silence is *a way* to avoid problems."

Saman had learned his lesson about silence some years before when he was writing textbooks for use in schools just after he graduated from university. He was part of a team of writers, and his team leader who had recently joined the team inquired about one of his lecturers at university over lunch. Everyone was in a lively mood during lunch, and it rubbed off on Saman as well. He knew all about Dr. Bakoon and his reputation with the women. His wife, a lecturer with the English department, was a rather reserved lady and absorbed in her work. They had a child, but it did not stop Bakoon from having several affairs. He kept them quiet, although the students gossiped about it.

Saman told his new team leader all he had heard about Bakoon. She asked him many questions, and he obliged answers according to what he knew and had heard. But he realized that his team leader was looking flustered and was a tad defensive about Bakoon's actions. "Perhaps they are just hearsay?" she interjected.

"Perhaps. But I've seen Dr. Bakoon often with so and so," Saman tried to back up his assessment of Bakoon. When they returned to the office, his colleagues told him that Bakoon and their new team leader were in a relationship! Saman was dumbfounded by what he heard. *Have I spoken too much?* he wondered.

In the next few weeks, the team worked on a topic about explorers. His team leader assigned Saman to research Zheng He, the great Chinese admiral and explorer, for a passage in the book.

Saman's team leader rejected every article about Zheng He that he found. "Is this the best article you can find?"

"I have looked at seven different articles," Saman answered as he pulled out the Xerox copies from his bag.

She took a cursory look at them and threw them back on the table. "I am afraid these are not what I want. Have you tried looking in the university library?"

Their team worked in one of the old houses of the Singapore University on Bukit Timah Road. The university had many small buildings that were converted to government offices by the authorities. The old university library was still available to trainee teachers.

Saman headed off to the library and began his search. He found nothing that looked better than the articles he already had. He asked the librarian for help but did not get much assistance. They were amid recataloging the books that they wanted to keep and packing the others to be shipped out.

After a couple of weeks of searching without success, his team leader threw him a lead. "Yesterday I mentioned it to Bakoon, and he suggested an encyclopedia in which a write-up on Zheng He can be found."

Saman felt the stab of her eyes as she threw him a look when she raised her head to look at him. He swore he detected a sarcastic smile on the corners of her mouth, but they soon disappeared.

"Do you have the title?" He sounded eager.

She detected it. "Oh, come on. Bakoon's a busy man. You're lucky he's even bothered to help. I'm afraid you have to look it up yourself."

Saman knew she was getting back at him for what he had said about her beau. He knew he should have kept his big mouth shut.

Setting off to the National Library in the city center, Saman cursed his luck. "Now she's always going to be on my case," he told himself. That was all that he thought about as he looked through the volumes of the encyclopedia. There were many publishers whose encyclopedias were referenced by the National Library. Finally, he found a couple of write-ups, and he took them back to his office.

"Now this looks like a suitable piece to go into our textbook," she quipped, giving him a cold stare. "Well, you'll still have to work with it so that it fits what we want."

Saman turned to head out of her office. Just before he exited through the old creaking door, he heard her victorious voice. "And don't you forget the exercises that need to accompany the passage," she called back.

That day, Saman learned that silence was the way to avoid problems. Over the years, as one by one of the other writers left the unit, she ensured that Saman stayed back to help her with getting the books ready to be submitted to the publisher.

When the unit had completed its project and disbanded, Saman joined the technology division as a trainer. His former team leader wrote to his director and requested Saman's help to proofread the manuscripts of the book as it went through its oxalic and bromide stages. These were part of the process of getting the book ready. They could still make changes until they submitted the bromides to the publishers. She had made sure that she extracted the last ounce of work out of him.

By then, Saman had started taking things in his stride, and he felt amused that he had got under her skin. She was a taskmaster, no doubt, but unwittingly and unintentionally, she had had her comeuppance. For Saman, it was a lesson that he never forgot. They did not see each other again after they published the book. Their scores were even.

Mysticism was yet another road toward his goal. The Vedic traditions began several thousand years ago. They had guided people who engaged in any activity only after consulting an astrologer or an almanac.

Saman had found some consolation in the belief. He learned that the yellow sapphire—*kanagapushparagam*, or *Pukhraj* stone—favored his zodiac sign. He had to start wearing it on a specific day after observing the necessary conditions between five and seven in the morning. Saman was not a mystic by any measure, but he had come to the realization that the many roads merged. He was not against them.

———————————

Saman chanced upon it. He was walking down a crowded street in a quarter of the city called Little India. Just after the canal that bordered the start of the road sat the huge Tekka Market. One could get almost anything there. The older folk frequented it, often with their daughter or son in tow. When the children grew up, having been initiated to the charm of the bustling marketplace by their parents, they continued the tradition although less frequently. But the tradition continued.

Little India was a tourist attraction. It was common to see many haversack-bearing curious foreign visitors haggling the price of an exotic talisman with the sales assistant of one of the many little stalls that lined the street on the opposite side, along the narrow paths that crisscrossed the main Serangoon Road.

Single and double-story shop houses lined either side of it. Eateries sat next to jewelers who were flanked by textile merchants who paraded their sea-sequinned glittering saris in their shop windows that were in themselves a sight to behold.

Saman was one of these children who had grown up to follow the tradition started by his elders. He was weaving his way through the hypnotic din created by the crowd. Saman felt as if he was being led along by the sights, sounds, and smells that came together, creating a unique experience that was a microcosm of that which one would experience in a busy street in Chennai, India. It was apt to refer to it as Little India. A street astrologer beckoned Saman, who ignored him and followed the din. A gust of wind that blew the dust on the street into a miniwhirlpool picked up a page from one of the stalls along the road; the vendors used it to wrap their wares. The piece of paper plastered itself against his foot as he stopped at a traffic junction. He tried to shake it off from his leg, but the wind held it fast. Saman grabbed it and shoved it into his pocket before moving on.

Little did he realize that he would move into a world he had hitherto known only through hearsay.

<hr/>

When Saman reached into his pocket for his train ticket before going through the turnstile at the Little India station, he pulled out the piece of paper that he had earlier stuffed into his pocket. He was fortunate to find a seat; it was the Deepavali season. Many last-minute shoppers were jostling with one another. Many were happy to get standing space after they managed to buy their groceries, many of which they could only buy in Little India.

As Saman snuggled into the corner seat, he decided to look at the paper that had stubbornly insisted on clinging to him. He smiled, recalling its persistence. The journey home was long. He was happy he had something to distract himself instead of catching himself inadvertently staring at the groin of a stranger standing in front of him, swinging from side to side as the train sped away down a tunnel.

"Do you know where you are going on your life journey?" the headline spoke to him. "Do not miss the chance to find out from your guardian angel." There was a contact email. Saman felt something unassuming about the advertisement that lured him to it. He read on and found out what the kanagapushparagam stone or the yellow sapphire could do for him. Saman was at a stage in his life where one road was as good as another. He made contact through the email, and that led to him wearing the yellow sapphire stone. It worked. On the first Thursday that he placed it on his finger, he won some money on a bet that he had wagered the day before. That win piqued his curiosity to find out more.

———

As Saman delved into the mysticism of the clairvoyant and astrology, he learned about another perspective to understanding life. The guardian angel messenger told him that she had instructions to wait until that exact date to unveil everything to him. She had a message for him from one of his ancestors who was watching over him. That ancestor was from the Flamel family. He was an internationally renowned scholar and one of the greatest alchemists of all. Saman recalled that he had come across someone with a similar name in one of the *Harry Potter* movies. Upon further investigation, he found out that such a person was not just a fictitious character but that he lived in France in the fourteenth century, and he was a famed alchemist who was the only known maker of the philosopher's stone, a legendary substance with incredible powers. In other words, the secret for transforming lead into gold! But also the secret to eternal life!

What a coincidence, thought Saman.

The wizard had appeared as a Luminous Spirit to a clairvoyant through Saman's guardian angel to convey a message to Saman, who was a descendant of his. It was incredible! It was a well-kept secret for centuries.

The Luminous Spirit had information about Saman's past lives. His bad luck seemed to be simply the result of a karmic debt: in a past life, he had committed acts that are having direct repercussions on his life now!

"In asking me to give you his protective talisman for free, he is providing you with the solution to your problem of chronic bad luck," the clairvoyant told Saman. "It's much more than a gift. It's a magical treasure that will cancel out your karmic debt to free you from the circle of bad luck that has entrapped you. An alchemical power forgotten for centuries has finally reappeared for *your happiness* and *your health*."

The clairvoyant told Saman, "The sacred alchemical knowledge of Flamel seemed to be lost forever after his mysterious disappearance in 1418. It was only during the Renaissance that my ancestors recovered the writings. My ancestors published a portion of the work of the alchemist. However, out of respect for his will, they took care to keep the magical secrets of Flamel for themselves and their descendants. In other words, my family is also connected to this strange and mysterious person, just as you are."

She continued, "To me, there's no doubt about it: this is not a matter of chance. It is divine providence. Because you know, as well as I do, that divine providence often acts through mysterious ways. Just like this message that I'm sending you today. I mean, do you think it's easy to say to someone, 'You're a descendant of Flamel the Alchemist who was a great wizard?' No, and it's not easy writing it to you either. That's why I'm giving you all the facts, exactly as they occurred. This way you can see for yourself that you have the opportunity of a lifetime here. And it arrived in the most curious of manners: the voice of divine providence.

"Yes, it's undoubtedly divine providence that gave me a sign that day. It doesn't happen very often. I was looking for some rare magical plants that I can only obtain from special herbalists. I was walking down the street when a little voice rang out inside my head. The voice told me to look to my right. I turned my head and saw a homeless man. I went over to him and put a little money in his cup. It was at that exact moment that the miracle occurred before my very eyes.

"The man raised his head toward me. His face was luminous, like the face of an angel. He said nothing, but I heard a voice tell me, 'You will receive a visit tonight from a friend who will reveal a secret to you.' Then he lowered his head. When he raised it again, I saw the face of a grateful man smiling at me.

"I was surprised by this apparition even though I'm used to this type of physical manifestation. I was about to move on. When I raised my head, I glimpsed a commemorative plaque on the house in front of which the homeless man was sitting: 'House of the Flamels.'

"I was in the neighborhood, in the street I know well, and yet I was standing in front of the house of Flamel, the great wizard, at the same time. It was as if I were there. That very night, the Luminous Spirit visited me. I was writing to a friend when, all of a sudden, a benevolent force took hold of me.

"I would have driven it away, except that I sensed all the goodness in the world. So I gave the spirit some room. My fingers automatically started typing on my keyboard. Here is what the Luminous Spirit wanted me to communicate to you."

A Message to Bring You Luck and Prosperity

My name is Flamel; I am the Great Alchemist. Your ancestors served me in the past. I have chosen you to locate my descendants.

The year is now 2020, according to your calendar. The time has come for me to let my direct and indirect descendants, who are worthy of receiving my secret, know that I haven't forgotten them! There are seven of them. Contact all seven and tell them about the Alchemical Arch of Luck.

Give my Alchemical Protective Talisman to my last descendant. It will cancel out the karmic debt that is driving away all the good luck. Give the Alchemical Arch of Luck to him as well.

I thank the angels who have allowed me to reach out to my descendants through you. Say that I understand the trials and tribulations of life for my seventh descendant.

On the date, I will communicate to you in your next dream. Write to my descendant and talk about our encounter and the others. In this way, I will be able to provide all of them with the help they need.

Thank you, my dear friend, for accompanying me on this mission that I have promised myself I will fulfill.

N. Flamel

Saman was astonished. *Anyone can write a message like that, claiming to be a messenger sent by my ancestors,* he thought to himself. "But it happened to me exactly like it happened to her! I was walking down the familiar street when a stranger beckoned me to him. And then the piece of paper that clung to me and linked me to this clairvoyant is just too much of a coincidence, surely," he mumbled aloud.

Saman learned that as soon as he receives his Alchemical Arch of Luck, he would start to feel beneficent energy flowing through him as if he were showering in good vibrations. That shower will cleanse his aura so that, very rapidly, curious but beneficial events would happen in his everyday life.

He might hear a little voice telling him to buy a lottery ticket, have premonitory dreams, or see visions of winning numbers on the pages of a magazine. But that was not all; there were infinite other ways that divine providence could choose to ensure his happiness.

The clairvoyant explained how the other six descendants had come upon a new life, "For a previous descendant of Nicolas Flamel, his fortune arrived in the form of a completely unexpected inheritance! For you, Saman, I see winnings in your future! So do you want to rid yourself of all your money problems? My angelic vision has shown me that your financial situation isn't exactly a delight. I sense that you have trouble making ends meet and that there is tension between you and your inner circle of family and friends due to a lack of resources. It is nothing to be ashamed of, Saman. The Alchemical Arch of Luck has the power to chase all dark forces, negative energy, and bad luck from your life forever!"

It was no coincidence either that as soon as Saman had acquired the kanagapushparagam stone, he won some money.

He had last won some money through games of chance three years ago, and then the stream just seemed to have dried up mysteriously.

Saman was excited by two turns of events. First, when he was able to control his mouth. He had started to exercise the feminine qualities he had inherited from his mother. They had lain dormant until now. It was such a joy to be able to help others feel good about themselves. He learned and was able to understand that his kindness and good deeds manifested themselves in the universe; it then came back to him manyfold.

The other was the discovery of another world, the world of mysticism. Saman grew up as a Christian; he saw the similarities between the two. While he was devout in his belief, he was not able to decide conclusively about the mystical world that he had now contacted.

"Why are you dabbling with these spirits?" his wife had expressed her anxiety. "I hope you do not get scammed by them and lose all your money again!" She had her justifications. If he ended up losing money to them, it would mean he had not learned his lesson.

"I am not dabbling in spirits." Yet he was aware that the clairvoyant had contacted him with a message from a Luminous Spirit. Saman felt a tinge of guilt.

If I am a devout Christian, does that mean that Buddha has nothing to teach me about life? Then why is it all right to learn about the great men in history? Shakespeare, Gandhi, Confucius? Saman had had this confusion for some time. But he had reached a stage in his life's journey when he came to understand that he could learn from everyone, anyone who had valuable lessons to teach him. Sadhguru had explained it as the moment of realization, not attainment. One could not attain something that had always been there inside of oneself. Such a realization was a humbling moment.

Saman liked the difference between realizing something and attaining something. Attainment related to the world outside of oneself. Materialistic pursuits, seeking love from someone else, or seeking the source of one's troubles in the external world were part of attainment. Realization, on the contrary, was about the world inside of oneself. Understanding, peace, and acceptance were examples of what one could find within oneself.

Having resolved to start searching himself *first*, Saman could appreciate the importance of understanding himself as the *starting point*. *"If I cannot control my thoughts, I cannot control my actions. Faith can indeed shape my thoughts and bring me to the abyss of change,"* Saman realized.

"I want to change. I want to be a better man. I want to live a more disciplined life. I obtain all the abundance that I create with my mind. Fortune and abundance magically manifest themselves because the magic is inside me. Money is energy, and the universe is abundant with energy. My mind is infinite and gives me infinite abundance and fortune. I use my abundance with love and generosity."

The thoughts reverberating in Saman's conscious mind were want, live, create, and use. They were all actions he would take. The faith he had in his thoughts could bring the change he wanted when he'd act. His consistent acts toward his goal were the key. Then these thoughts would set in his subconscious mind, and he would act habitually. He would be a new man. He could be anything he wanted, and he desired to lead a better life for himself and others.

It was no different from what he had wanted all along. The difference, though, was the focus. Saman had strayed from his goal in life. Life had the tendency to do that, he realized. Saman recalled the words of Lennon: "Life is what happens to you when you're busy making other plans."

"I paid little attention to the daily things that moved me little by little away from my goal. I got lost in the outside world. It was great when I immersed myself in one thing after another, but it is the focus that can get you ahead in life. I should have said no when it mattered!" That was one thing he learned he had to do. If you want something in life, it is within easy reach, but can you concentrate on what you want and ignore everything else that distracts?

When Andrew Carnegie faced a commission of inquiry set up to investigate how he had amassed his immense wealth, they found nothing to incriminate him. So they asked him, "Tell us, Mr. Carnegie, how did you manage to do it?"

"Can you concentrate on one thing for five minutes?" he replied.

Saman was thinking about the actions he would take to realize his goal of becoming a better person. As he stared blankly at the shimmering water in the afternoon sun, an idea flashed across his mind.

Years before, a speaker at a conference he was attending advised that he had to do what was right. He suddenly got an insight into what doing the right thing meant. To do the right thing, he just had to listen to the voice inside him. That voice would always echo the values that were dear to him.

"Believe nothing, no matter where you read it or who has said it, not even if I have said it unless it agrees with your reason and your common sense," said Gautama.

I have reasoned to myself and filtered what I have learned through my values and my common sense. To do what is right, I have to act by following my values, Saman thought to himself.

In his work, he realized that doing the right thing meant acting according to the values of the organization. At home, it meant acting according to the values held by his family.

Saman felt a surge of confidence in himself. *Nobody can tell you what is right. You have to realize it yourself.* It took Saman thirty years ever since he had been pondering the question in his mind. He was happy because now he knew.

"Knowing anything is nothing. You need to act accordingly, then it will be something." Saman turned his head to look around him, but he was alone. It was that same voice from inside him that had spoken.

"I have to act! I have to focus on what my thoughts tell me to do, and I have to concentrate. That single-minded dedication and passion will bring me closer to my goal," Saman spoke to himself.

"Where were you all day long?"

"I was just downstairs at the pool. It is serene out there. What have you been doing?"

"I have a million things to do. I plan to read this book that you lent to me. I have to write out the business plan for the project that Joel and I are thinking of starting. And I have to find out about the National Service that begins for me in February."

"You know—" Saman began.

"No. Not another one of your lectures, Dad, please."

Saman smiled and continued. "Multitasking is the biggest scam unleashed on people."

"What are you saying?"

"Multitasking is like being a jack of all trades but master of none. It is an invention of corporations to get people to do many things at one time. It keeps them busy. They have no time to think. Worst of all, they do not focus on anything."

"So why is it a scam?"

"Multitasking is good for the organization."

"So there is no problem then?"

"Not quite. Multitasking for years makes it almost automatic for the individual. It means his habit is to do many things without focusing on any single task."

"And?"

"He loses the ability to concentrate on any one thing for an extended period."

"Why does he need to do that if he can do so many things at the same time?"

"Look, it's like this. If you want to make your business a success, you have to concentrate on it. You cannot let anything else take precedence. With that kind of focus, you will succeed." Saman smiled at his son, who looked at him quizzically. Saman knew at once that no matter how much he explained, the boy would have to go through his journey in life and come to realize what was important to him.

"Okay, Dad, I've got to go now to meet Joel. You take care, and don't get your head all muddled up with the stuff you've been watching lately on YouTube."

"You be careful too." As Saman watched his son leave, he wondered what would become of him. He was all grown up now. He remembered when he held him in his arms—how little and fragile he seemed. He was now getting ready for National Service in two months, to defend the country, his family, and his friends.

"He will be all right," that voice from inside assured him.

Saman was not one to save much money. He liked to spend what he earned. He lived for today, although he always aspired to be well provided for in the future. The lack of money was one of his biggest problems; the other was love. He decided to act on the first problem first.

"Let me try out a simple project. I want to start saving money. I shall put aside one hundred dollars every day. At the end of the month, I should have $3,000." Of course, he had $3,000 with him, and he could immediately achieve his goal.

What Saman wanted to do was to cultivate the habit of saving. He needed the discipline to go through the routine of taking out one hundred dollars from his wallet or his account and go through the physical act of putting it aside.

I will not open another account, for now, to save this money. After all, the banks are paying pittance as interest. Did I not read that in some countries they have negative interest rates? It means that I have to pay them to keep my money. It may be safe with them, but banks do wind up, don't they? he ruminated.

If he succeeded, he would have subscribed to an idea suggested by another financial guru: pay yourself first. Saman was serious about his goal.

That day was November 19. He counted the days using his fingers, and by December 18, he would have reached his first goal. He had a purse the size of half a page given to him by an old friend with several dividers in them. He decided to put his savings in there. The pocket with the zipper was where he put his first one hundred dollars. As an afterthought, he put in another fifty dollars into one of the other dividers. "It could come in handy," he convinced himself. Saman was pleased with his effort.

On the following days, Saman woke up earlier than usual. He was excited about the goal he set for himself. After his morning ablutions, he devoted an hour to his daily prayers.

Even though Saman had an open mind to all faiths and teachings, he was, most of all, a devout believer of his faith.

In his present state of mind, he felt he was better disposed to focusing on his goal. Saman took out his purse and put in his second one hundred dollars, then he slotted in another fifty dollars into the divider where he had put fifty dollars yesterday. It was the first time in his life he had kept to a resolution until the second day! Everything seemed to be going well. Saman looked at the contents of the purse, and he was pleased.

Saman took his phone out from his pocket. He pulled out the notepad and started calculating the dates and the amount of money he would have set aside in a year:

18/12	3,000
17/01	3,000
16/02	3,000
18/03	3,000
17/04	3,000
17/05	3,000
16/06	3,000
16/07	3,000
15/08	3,000
14/09	3,000
14/10	3,000
14/11	3000
Total	36,000

Saman was more pleased with himself and was committed to staying the course. He focused on his goal in his mind. He visualized each date and the amount of money he would have. He saw the $36,000 in his mind's eye, focused on it, and said to himself, "By November 14 next year, I will have saved $36,000."

Saman then started setting his yearly goals until he reached his first $1,000,000.

Saman stayed true to his plan to build his savings nest egg without thinking much about it. It was now becoming a routine that he was getting used to, but it was not a habit yet, he reminded himself. It would not be one until he'd reach his first target.

⋯◆⋯

Soon it was the twelfth of December. Saman looked into his purse to check that the money was there. He kept it in the bottom drawer of the cabinet in his bedroom. Only he, his wife, and his younger boy used the room. His younger son used to lie on Saman's bed when he was not using it. His son had seen him pull the drawer out, but he had not asked Saman anything about it.

Saman was surprised to find $2,400 in the zipped pocket of the purse. There was $1,200 in the divider into which he had put fifty dollars every day and an additional $1,380 in another pocket. He had a total of $4,980, one week ahead of his first target!

The additional fifty dollars a day that he had put aside without counting toward his target had helped him get to it earlier. The other extra money was the winnings from his small wager. He had put it into another of the dividers in the purse. Saman had told himself that he would not spend any of his winnings since he was already spending money on placing his frequent bets, though he wagered them for the fun of it. *I am not a gambler. It is just like the festive card games I play with my family and friends*, Saman consoled himself.

Saman was delighted to see the sum of money he had saved. He remembered reading the six rules of money stated in *The Richest Man in Ancient Times*. It was referring to gold, but it applied to money as well. Two of the rules he mentioned were about savings and about learning from those who knew more about money: gold comes to the man who puts at least one-tenth of his earnings aside and gold comes to the man who listens to those who know more about it than himself.

Saman used to earn a lot more money before, but he did not put much away for a rainy day. Now he hardly had as much, but he had set a goal to save first and then to spend what he had left.

The rules of money certainly seemed to be working. Saman had reached his first goal of $3,000, and he had done it before the end of thirty days. Moreover, money seemed to come from nowhere to him. Money sought him out; perhaps it felt that Saman was ready to cherish it, keep it, and multiply it. Most significant of all, Saman was still the generous, caring, and kind person that he had always been; it was just that he was kind to himself as well.

Saman experienced the exhilaration of meeting the first financial goal he had set. *I can achieve anything I want. Now for my next goal.* Saman was in the zone in his mind. He wanted to keep experiencing the burst of energy he felt. It was good. No, it was great.

———————

"Happy birthday!" The greeting reverberated in the living room as he entered it. He had woken up to get some water from the refrigerator. He had had the same dream again. Shadows were dancing on the beige walls of the living room, and Saman was not sure if he was still dreaming. Saman rubbed his eyes with his forefingers and surveyed the room. His family was there; his wife was holding a cake with a few candles burning brightly on it.

"What time is it?"

"It is midnight. Happy birthday!" the family members answered in one voice.

"Thank you. But why at this hour? I got a fright, as I just had a dream and wanted to get some water."

Nobody was paying attention to what he said. "Come and blow out the candles, make a wish, and cut the cake." They were more eager than he was. Saman half-staggered toward the dining table and did as instructed.

"What's your birthday wish, Dad?" his sons asked him.

He managed a smile at them. "You will find out soon, I hope."

"May all your wishes come true," they all echoed together. Again, Saman smiled at them. After they had eaten a slice of cake each, they went back to bed. Saman sat alone on the sofa, thinking.

"It is time to change course," he said aloud. Then he continued thinking. Soon he was deep in his thoughts, and he dozed off.

"Go, Saman. Go. Have no fear. You can do it." They were still hoping he'd take the next step. He could barely make out their faces. There was his father; his neighbor, Uncle Ryan; and his father's siblings, Samboo Atthai his aunt and Uncle Louis.

"If you fly, you'll soar!" "If you fly, you'll soar!" And they looked at him expectantly, urging him to let go and trust himself.

Samboo atthai, his father's sister, was his favorite aunt. She lived in Bekok, a small town about an hour away by train from Kluang. Saman loved visiting her. Surrounding her wooden house were all kinds of tropical fruit trees, from durian, guava, rambutan, mangosteen, mango to star fruit. A long fence covered with betel nut leaves separated the railway tracks from the house. Samboo atthai loved to chew on the betel nut leaf, usually just after lunch. She had an empty

Jacob's biscuit tin in which she kept the condiments for her after-lunch ritual.

"Go and pluck two leaves for me. Let's see if you know how to pick the best," Samboo atthai would tell Saman. As a little boy, he loved running errands for her. As he handed her the two leaves, he surveyed her face to see if she approved of his choice.

Samboo Atthai knew he was waiting for a sign from her. She first wiped the leaves on the sarong at her lap as she sat down on the cool cement floor at the entrance of the house. The view had a calming effect. One could see the trees swaying in the wind; there was always a cool breeze blowing that mitigated the heat of the afternoon sun. Before long, a train would sound its horns as it pulled into the railway station that was walking distance from the house.

Saman watched as his aunt then spread some chunam or lime chalk on the leaf and placed two pieces of a sliced betel nut on it. She then folded it into a cone and stuffed it into her mouth. As she chewed on it, her lips reddened, and Saman waited anxiously as his aunt expertly placed the first two fingers of her right hand on her lips and sent a stream of red liquid shooting directly into the drain that made a perimeter around the house. She never seemed to miss.

Aunt Samboo looked satisfied as she gave her verdict, "Excellent!" Saman was pleased with himself.

Aunt Samboo was an excellent cook. Saman enjoyed her cooking, although it was spicy enough to get his eyes tearing. Immediately after eating her delicious curry, he would stick his tiny hands into the sugar jar, grab a handful of sugar in his fist, and artfully release a stream of sugar into his mouth. He tilted his head upward, held his fist above his mouth, and with his tearing eyes closed, he could get the sugar into his mouth.

Aunt Samboo and Saman shared a special bond. She was expecting her first child when Saman's mother was pregnant with him. Aunt Samboo delivered a week before his mother, but her baby girl was stillborn.

As tears rolled down her face, she would hold the newborn Saman in her lap and sing lullabies to him. To her, Saman was her baby. Saman's father adored his sister and told Saman's mother not to stop her if it helped her overcome her grief.

Aunt Samboo soon got over her loss. She adopted a son and doted on him. Still, Saman was always special to her. All of a sudden, she died on a fateful day unexpectedly.

<hr />

"Is everyone ready? We have about half an hour to make it to church," someone called out. Everyone in Saman's house was getting ready to attend his cousin's wedding. The house was bursting with energy, and a mix of musk and floral scents filled the air.

It was a sunny afternoon in December 1988. Saman's cousin, the last but one daughter of his father's brother, Uncle Louis, was getting married. Samboo atthai had also come over to attend the wedding ceremony. She had made the trip down from Singapore, where she now lived.

Earlier that morning, all the ladies of the two households, determined to look their best, headed to the hairdresser's at the main road, a stone's throw from the house. Samboo atthai also decided to join the entourage as they made a procession to the shop.

When they returned home, beads of sweat started forming on Samboo atthai's forehead and face. She dismissed it because of the walk under the sun from the shop back to the house. The others were busying themselves trying to look resplendent in the new saris and dresses they had bought for the occasion. They did not notice what was happening with her at first.

"Hurry. Someone fetch a glass of water. Aunt Samboo is frothing at her mouth," one of the cousins hollered. She had a heart attack. Soon word was sent by one of Saman's cousins to his house, which was just one street away.

Saman rushed to his cousin's house. Aunt Samboo was lying motionless on a bed on the floor. There were many people in the room. Saman spoke to his uncle Louis and his eldest cousin brother, "Let me handle this. You go ahead with the wedding. She will be all right."

Uncle Louis looked troubled. Aunt Samboo was his little sister, and he loved her. She was the life of the party whenever they had a gathering. She was looking forward to the wedding, and now this had happened.

Saman and his uncle Louis exchanged a knowing look. Uncle Louis was a father figure to him and his family ever since Saman's father had passed away. Saman assured his uncle that he would take care of everything and rushed Samboo atthai to the Kluang General Hospital.

When the car pulled into the lobby of the hospital, Saman and his brother met some friends who worked there, and they knew Aunt Samboo well. Kluang was a small town after all, and everyone knew everyone else. Saman thanked the doctor and nurses who attended to his aunt immediately. Soon she was receiving help.

Saman sat on the bench outside the ward. *What a day!* he thought. *Why did someone not stop Samboo atthai from going to the hairdresser's? This unfortunate incident would not have taken place. I hope everything is going to be all right.*

"Your aunt's condition is under control. Don't worry," one of the nurses reported to Saman after almost an hour.

"Can I see her? Please?" Saman appealed to the nurse.

She pursed her lips and looked back into the ward at the sister who was in charge, who nodded her head. "All right, just five minutes. There's nothing you can do. So do not disturb the patient unnecessarily."

Saman spoke to Samboo atthai. "You are going to be all right. They are all people we know, and they will take good care of you," Saman said as he gestured with his head toward the nurses who were busy with the other patients.

Tears rolled down Samboo atthai's cheeks. Saman placed his palm on her wrist and told her that he would be waiting outside. His aunt's eyes moved to her left as she looked at him one last time.

"Please go back. We will keep you informed. It is an intensive care ward, and you cannot be here. I hope you understand."

Saman left for home; it was the last he saw his Samboo atthai alive.

————— ◆ —————

The telephone rang at Saman's house. His mother looked at him; she wore a frown on her face. Saman looked at the clock. It was eightish.

"Who could that be?" his mother read his mind. They were hoping it was not about who they thought it was. Saman took the call. It was his uncle Louis's wife, Aunt Louisa.

"Samboo atthai has left us," she wailed into the phone. Saman turned to look at his mother; she had tears in her eyes. Somehow she knew. Saman shook his head; his mother understood what he dreaded to repeat.

The two households got together to commiserate with each other. "We did not expect this to happen," Uncle Louis's wife said to Saman. She thought he was upset that Samboo atthai did not get immediate attention two days ago when she had had a heart attack.

Saman had thought about it then, but he was not unreasonable. He understood that amid a wedding going on in less than an hour, anyone would waver. They did; he understood.

Uncle Louis walked into the living room. Saman hugged him, and they both cried on each other's shoulders. The two men did not utter any words; there was no need for that. Uncle Louis was the oldest brother of Saman's dad. Saman was now the head of his household, taking the place of his dad. He felt what his uncle Louis felt.

Uncle Louis had Samboo atthai buried according to Hindu custom. She remained a Hindu, while her brothers had converted to Christianity when Saman's dad married. He followed his wife's religion so as not to confuse the children they would have later. Uncle Louis followed suit after he and his wife had prayed for their son and God answered their prayers.

After Saman's dad died, Uncle Louis made sure that his brother's family was all right. Every day, Saman's mother would take a bowl of curry that she had prepared to Uncle Louis's house. He had insisted that she did so. It was his way of staying informed about what his brother's children were eating every day. Uncle Louis was a loving and kind man. He loved Saman and his siblings, and they never felt the absence of their father too deeply because Uncle Louis was always there for them.

On occasion, when the children got out of line, he would admonish them. He never held it against them, and they did not bear any grudge against him. It was like being punished by their father.

Once, when Saman was a teenager, he had argued with his uncle Louis about a trivial matter. Before he knew it, he felt a hot flash on his face as his uncle's arm swung at him. He felt a ringing sound in his ear and never forgot the lesson. But

Uncle Louis was also a humorous man; the children loved to tease him, and they enjoyed his wit and humor. However, he was a stickler when it concerned showing respect for elders, regardless. Saman loved his uncle Louis; it hurt him that he had overstepped the line. The next day, Uncle Louis invited him over to his house and insisted that Saman took his meal there. Saman was happy; he was worried that his uncle would still be angry with him. He knew that things were back to normal, and all was forgiven but not forgotten.

Saman looked up to his uncle Louis. He worked as a technician, and with his income, he managed his family and made sure they did not want for anything. It was not a luxurious life, but it was sufficient.

Uncle Louis was active in church; he was a warden during Sunday mass. He dressed his best on Sundays, and it was indeed the day for feasting in the house after Sunday mass. Saman's aunt Louisa served the best dishes of the week on Sundays. It was the same in Saman's household.

When Saman and his siblings went to school, Uncle Louis and his wife made sure that the children lived with them for some time. That way, they would get the same attention as Uncle Louis's children; they all sat at the ten-foot dinner table before dinner to revise their schoolwork every day without fail between seven and nine in the evening. They ate their dinner after that.

Saman and his siblings had deep respect and admiration for Uncle Louis and his wife. They were both like surrogate parents to them. When Saman's siblings got married, Uncle

Louis and his wife always sat at the main table together with Saman's mother. It was their way of showing their respect and gratitude to them. Uncle Louis loved it. He felt a sense of pride that his brother's children had grown up the right way.

When he was eighty-nine years old, he passed away. He had been looking forward to celebrating his ninetieth birthday grandly, but it was not to be. He had lived a long, fulfilling, and meaningful life. The entire clan was there to give him a deserving send-off. Saman's cousins asked him to give the eulogy at Uncle Louis's funeral.

"Bon voyage, Uncle Louis. We shall meet again. Thank you for everything you have done for my family. We love you."

As the undertakers lowered Uncle Louis into his grave, Saman recalled the special moments that they had shared. Uncle Louis treated Saman like his son.

"Remember. If you can, look after Mark," Uncle Louis said to Saman one day when Saman called on him just before he passed away. Mark was Uncle Louis's son. Saman recalled the glint in his eyes from the moisture in them as he spoke those words. Despite the facade, he was a tenderhearted man. He was just being tough for everyone as the head of the family.

Saman did not forget.

Mark was several years older than Saman. Mark was the fun-loving type, and in his youth, he had often got himself involved in an affray with his friends. Nevertheless, Mark was intelligent and worldly-wise. The rest of his siblings toed the line and, as a result, were more mainstream in their views. Mark, however, was unconventional in his outlook on life.

Mark started smoking when he was eighteen. He had a hobby of collecting different brands of cigarettes, and he displayed them in the glass cabinet in the house.

Saman and his cousins used to read the brand names and often played games where they challenged one another to give examples of different categories—such as animals, cars, fruits, cigarettes, and countries—that started with a letter of the alphabet that one of them called out. They spent many hours entertaining themselves in these games.

Saman and his friends were innovative. They created their games, including designing board games, since they could not afford the board games sold at the Emporium in town.

Saman used the cardboard back of a drawing block. He would first cover it with white paper and then create his board games. One such game was a Grand Prix Circuit, complete with pit stops that stalled the progress of the players as well as the opportunity to move forward several places if one landed on a suitable slot. For tokens, he used pebbles or used tamarind seeds. He shaved the top of the covering off and used a marker pen to write names similar to tokens used in Monopoly: car, dog, ship, and iron. For a dice, he sliced an eraser into a cube and used a ballpoint pen to write the numbers from 1 to 6.

Saman was not good at art. He got the help of his friends to draw the background depicting a racetrack and had it colored. The children in the neighborhood congregated at Saman's house for hours. Their parents did not mind, as it kept the children engaged and away from mischief.

Saman and his cousins did get into some mischief, though. At night while the rest of the household was asleep, the urchins experimented with the cigarettes. Each night they would smoke one brand. At first they choked on the smoke, as they were not used to the smoke. But soon they became quite good at inhaling and exhaling the smoke. The boys were careful. They would light the cigarette and press their faces against the metal grille covering the open window as they blew the smoke out into the night air.

Nobody realized the mischief the boys were up to until one day. They were all doing spring-cleaning in preparation for Christmas. The boys joined their female cousins. One of the girls was cleaning the glass cabinet. "Some of the boxes are empty!" she cried out. Her shrill voice was enough to alert the older cousins, who seemed to always be on the lookout to see if the younger boys had got into any mischief.

"Yes. It's empty," one of Saman's older female cousins verified after checking the boxes. The boys had put the empty boxes back in the glass display cabinet, hoping that no one would notice, but this time someone did.

Soon an investigation was mounted by Aunt Louisa. Naturally, the boys were the first suspects. They looked guilty too. Their faces gave them away.

"Look at their eyes," another older cousin remarked. The boys tried desperately to change their facial expressions. They swore their innocence.

"Where did the cigarettes disappear?" Aunt Louisa and the rest questioned Saman and his two male cousins.

"Mark must be the one who smoked them," one of the boys suggested. Mark was now working in a nearby town with an oil palm plantation. He had living quarters there and returned home once a fortnight when he had a couple of days off from work.

"All right, we will ask Mark when he gets back next week," Aunt Louisa declared. The boys were off the hook, but they were not free from suspicion. They heaved a sigh of relief.

When Mark returned the following week, the adjourned investigation resumed. "Mark, do these packets belong to you?" Aunt Louisa asked, gesturing with her upturned chin pointed in the direction of the glass cabinet.

Mark suspected that something was amiss. "Yes. Why do you ask, mom?"

"The boys claim that you must be the one who took the cigarettes from the boxes." She was careful not to say that Mark smoked, although she knew of his habit. Mark looked at the boys and then at his mother.

"Yes, I think so," he replied casually and headed for the bathroom to take his shower. He had rescued the boys. In the evening, when the boys were playing a board game, Mark joined them. "What game are you playing?" he asked as he wedged himself between two boys on the floor. "I did not smoke those cigarettes. I know you must be the culprits. I want you to stop, starting today. Do you understand?" He looked sternly at Saman and his two younger brothers.

"Yes," they replied in unison, and Mark left them to continue their game. The boys looked sheepishly at one another. Their cigarette-smoking escapade ended then and there. They were grateful they had the understanding of an older sibling. Mark was like an older sibling to Saman.

Many years later, whenever Saman visited Kuala Lumpur for work or on holiday, he would look Mark up. They enjoyed each other's company and spoke freely to each other. They discussed many things of interest: sports, music, women, business, and their friends and family.

"How's life treating you these days?" Mark, who had now retired from his work at a well-known hotel, inquired.

"I'm fine, *anneh*." Saman always addressed Mark as his older brother. "How have you been keeping? I heard that you have just returned from a jazz festival in Hua Hin?" Saman said.

"Yes, it's amazing stuff, great music, with everyone in a relaxed mood," Mark replied. "You know Thailand, a great place for a holiday. You must join me one of these days."

Mark was a jazz music enthusiast and often invited his younger cousin along. Saman loved his music; he enjoyed rock and roll and pop music more. He was only now beginning to take an interest in jazz music.

"Yes, I will."

"We'll have a great time at the music festival. There's one coming up soon in Jakarta. It's your kind of place, isn't it?" Mark said, laughing. Mark knew that Saman frequented Indonesia, as he had several good friends there.

Before they parted company, Saman pushed a few dollar bills into Mark's hands. Mark refused to accept them.

"Just keep them for your weekly tipple and a smoke, anneh," Saman said. After some persuasion, Mark accepted it. Mark had money; he did not need any money from Saman. Growing up, they had cultivated the habit by watching their uncles and aunts do the same with their elders. Saman and Mark just kept up the old practice.

They loved each other. One could tell from the fondness each displayed in the other's company. The freedom with which they spoke about anything that interested them was also evident. They did not hold anything back. Saman always looked up to Mark and valued his insights and advice. Mark had seen more of the world than Saman; and he was, after all, like his older brother.

When Mark was asking after the rest of the family, he mentioned Uncle Ryan, who had recently passed away. Uncle Ryan was their neighbor. He lived next door to Uncle Louis, and they worked at the same place.

Saman and his cousins were friends with Uncle Ryan's children. He had six boys. Appu, Uncle Ryan's second son, was Saman's best friend, and Saman often spent many hours at the Ryans'.

Uncle Ryan was a contemporary of Saman's dad. Uncle Louis was about twelve years older than them. Uncle Ryan, like Saman's dad, was interested in sports. They shared a passion for badminton and football. Saman's dad was the Kluang District badminton champion in the 1960s. As a five-year-old, Saman remembered sitting up to wait for his dad to return home after his thrice-weekly badminton practice. He would often get home past midnight. A sleepy-eyed Saman would sit up and watch his dad practice skipping to build up his stamina. After that, he would shower and eat a light meal before retiring to bed.

Uncle Ryan would be doing the same thing next door. When Saman was older, he and the neighbor's children took after their parents and enjoyed playing badminton. Sometimes Uncle Ryan would join in, although he was much older by then. The children did not let up whenever they played against their fathers or their uncles. It was very competitive, and soon the boys were representing their respective schools at the district championships.

"Where's Saman?" Uncle Ryan would inquire of his family if he did not see Saman around the house for some time. He was fond of his good friend's son.

When Saman appeared at his house, Uncle Ryan would invite him for a cup of tea. Uncle Ryan was a seasoned tea drinker. He always had an aluminum teapot filled with tea sitting on the table in front of him when he returned from work or on weekends.

He was often bare-bodied, wearing only his sarong. "Nahah," Uncle Ryan would call out to his wife, who instinctively placed a cup of tea for Saman. She often gave Uncle Ryan a cross look because she was busy preparing lunch for everyone when he interrupted her. Uncle Ryan would respond with a smile, and Aunt Nahah would complain to Saman about Uncle Ryan.

"See for yourself, Saman, how busy I am. I have no girls to give me a helping hand. This man and his six sons are always making requests of me. How many hands do they think I have?" she would say to Saman, half-smiling. Uncle Ryan would let out a laugh and then break out in a coughing spasm. He was a chain-smoker who swore by his Rough Rider cigarettes.

Aunt Nahah made a mean cup of tea. Years later, Saman would still be singing her praises to his wife whenever he had tea. "Nobody makes tea like Aunt Nahah. The tea was of the right temperature, and the milk and sugar were in the correct proportion. It was not thick like the tea in the coffee shops. It was light but right," Saman would reminisce. He missed Aunt Nahah's tea.

Uncle Ryan and Aunt Nahah were a loving couple. They liked Saman. Uncle Saman often engaged the boy in conversation, as he was knowledgeable about many things, like sports. Aunt Nahah considered Saman like her seventh son.

Every Deepavali, the Hindu festival of lights, Saman was the first guest at the Ryans'. Uncle Ryan and Aunt Nahah would invite him over for breakfast, and Saman would join their children for steaming hot *idlis* or *dosa* and piping hot chicken curry to dip the idlis and dosa. They would douse it all down with a hot cup of tea.

"Eat to your heart's fill, Saman," Uncle Ryan would say. Then turning to his wife, he would call out, "Nahah." She instinctively obliged by adding two more pieces of idlis to Saman's plate and ladling the chicken curry over them. "Enjoy, Saman," she would say with a smile on her face.

The boys ate until they had to release the buckle on the front of their trousers so that their tummies could fill out comfortably. Uncle Ryan and Aunt Nahah would look pleased.

Uncle Ryan often regaled Saman with stories about his friendship with Saman's dad. He especially loved recounting the time when they played football together. Uncle Ryan was a good footballer; Saman's dad was not. Still, he insisted on being part of the team, and so they often assigned the goalkeeping task to him, Uncle Ryan said. Then he would burst out into a loud guffaw as he recounted what had happened and then go into his coughing spasms again. "You know, Saman, your dad was a terrible footballer. We put him in goal so that he would not give the ball away. He ended up letting in a bucketful of goals instead." They would all burst out laughing.

When Saman's father died, Saman was devastated. He was preparing for his Lower Certificate of Education examinations in October. His dad died in September. When news reached them that Saman's dad was not going to pull through, a neighbor rushed him to the hospital, hoping that Saman could see his dad before he passed away. As Saman was running down the corridor to the ward, he heard shouts coming from that direction. He recognized the voices of his mother and sister. When Saman rushed to his dad's bedside, he had just died, and his body was still warm. Saman was inconsolable.

When they all returned home from the hospital, it was close to midnight. As Saman got out of the car, he saw Uncle Ryan standing outside the entrance to Uncle Louis's house. Saman's siblings and some close friends had also gathered there when they heard the devastating news. Saman recalled that Uncle Ryan was the first person to console him. Saman buried his head in Uncle Ryan's chest and cried out, "My dad is dead, Uncle Ryan."

Uncle Ryan looked visibly moved too, as he had lost his good buddy, who was only forty-two years old. "I'll always be here for you, Saman. Don't cry. You have to shoulder your dad's responsibilities and look after your mom and siblings," Uncle Ryan tried to give him the strength to man up to his predicament. That day, Saman became a man.

Uncle Ryan loved food. Saman was studying in Batu Pahat after he had completed his Malaysian Certificate of Education, the equivalent of the GCE O Level examinations conducted by the Cambridge Examinations Syndicate. Uncle Ryan would tell him stories about the best biryani he had eaten. It was by Jubilee Restaurant during the wedding reception of Saman's parents.

"The aroma would stick to the hands for hours," he recounted as his mouth watered just thinking about it. "That was almost nineteen years ago. All the other stalls sold fake biryani," Uncle Ryan protested.

"There's a famous biryani stall in Batu Pahat, Uncle Ryan. I'll get a packet of rice for you on my next weekend back home."

"You do that, and I will tell you how it compares with the biryani from Jubilee Restaurant that your dad served on his wedding day."

Saman bought a packet and brought it to Uncle Ryan, who was looking forward to it. More importantly, he was happy that Saman took the trouble on his behalf. After Uncle Ryan had taken a few mouthfuls, he turned to look at Saman. "It is tasty, but it does not measure up to that biryani."

Saman burst out laughing. He knew that the old master chefs were no longer around, and it was difficult for the new cooks to replicate the authentic taste of their biryani. Still, Uncle Ryan finished the packet of rice so as not to disappoint the boy.

When Saman moved to Singapore to work, he saw Uncle Ryan and his family less often, but he made it a point to call on them every time he was back in Kluang.

Uncle Ryan had retired by then, and he moved out of the government quarters where he was staying. He bought a terrace house in the same housing estate as Uncle Louis. Saman's mother and siblings were staying in a rental house one street away from Uncle Louis and about a fifteen-minute walk from Uncle Ryan's house.

Whenever Saman called on Uncle Ryan and Aunt Nahah, they were delighted. Their conversations often picked up from where they had last left it.

"So tell me, when are you getting married?" Uncle Ryan would inquire. He knew Saman and Jay were engaged to be married soon. Saman once brought Jay along with him when he visited Uncle Ryan and Aunt Nahah. "Don't forget to invite me. I will not miss it for anything," Uncle Ryan told Saman, and he did not.

Uncle Ryan attended Saman's wedding and stayed at the bridegroom's residence on the wedding day. He joined in the merrymaking, and he later told Saman that it was not since the wedding of Saman's dad that he had enjoyed himself as much. Saman's friends, family, and Uncle Ryan were, of course, happily drowned in spirits.

When Uncle Ryan passed away, Saman cried uncontrollably, sitting beside his body covered in flowers.

Aunt Nahah sat at his foot, and she was trying to console Saman. Saman had not cried as much for anybody since his dad died. He was an adult now, but he could not control the sobs that came from deep within his bowels.

Uncle Ryan was indeed someone Saman loved dearly, and his passing left an indelible mark on Saman. Saman knew that Uncle Ryan would continue to be there for him, just as he had told Saman on the day when Saman's father had died.

After the Hindu cremation ceremony, Saman comforted Aunt Nahah before he took his leave. "Don't forget to visit me when you are back in town, just because your Uncle Ryan is no longer around." She finally broke down. Saman hugged her.

Sadly, some years later, she passed on too, but Saman was at a conference overseas and could not attend her funeral. When he returned to Singapore, he made it a point to call on the Ryans to pay his respects and to offer his commiserations. They were holding the traditional sixteenth-day prayers for the repose of Aunt Nahah's soul. The Ryan siblings insisted that Saman be part of the prayer ceremony that her children had to perform. He was the seventh member.

———————◆◆◆———————

Saman recognized the voices he heard in his recurring dream. It was his dad, Samboo atthai, Uncle Louis, and Uncle Ryan. *Are they the ones watching over me that my mother had reminded me?* Saman wondered.

But they were not the only ones. Saman had dreamed of others he did not recognize. He had not seen them before. Yet they were all there like spectators at a sports meet, cheering him on as he ran the race of his life. They wanted him to win. They knew he could. Each had imparted their values to Saman through their interactions with him.

The clairvoyant had told him about Flamel, whom she claimed was one of his ancestors. *Is he among the spectators?* Saman felt a strange feeling come over him. *Did I hear a voice say something?* He was not afraid, though. Saman knew he could achieve anything he set his mind to; he had already experienced a small success.

This time around, Saman decided that his goal had to be life-changing for him. He also knew that he had to use the talents he already possessed and not be distracted by what other people were doing.

"What am I good at?" he wondered aloud. He heard a voice tell him, "Do what you have been doing all this while."

But he was not happy doing what other people wanted him to do, and he had been an educator for thirty-six years.

Do more of the same? He could not see how doing the same thing would be life-changing. "Did Einstein not say that doing the same thing but expecting the result to be different was insanity?" Saman felt that he should not rush into it this time. When he first started working, it was out of necessity to support his family. He did not have the luxury of being picky about it. He picked being a teacher; the money was good, and he liked showing other people how to do things.

Saman decided to sleep on it, and when he awoke, he would make up his mind.

Saman slept soundly that night. He did not dream of anything or hear anyone's voice. He felt good. He knew he had to make up his mind about what he wanted to do.

Saman switched on the television, and a documentary about the universe was on the air.

"It is just matter, space, time, and energy," the narrator's voice said. Saman felt he had read this somewhere before. *The universe is matter and energy set in time and space.* The thought kept flashing across his mind. Everything that he could feel or see and touch was matter. It existed in time and space. But had everything that he could feel, see, and touch always existed?

Just then, his phone rang. His attention was drawn to it by its vibrations. Saman had put the phone on silent mode, but he had activated the "vibrate on silent" mode.

Saman did not take the call. He was suddenly fascinated by the vibrating phone. He could feel it, but he could not see or touch the vibrations. It was energy. The vibrations were the atoms in motion, reverberating, and they created sound, which he neither could see nor touch, although he could hear it.

These things were not new, but they had a newness to him now. Saman was concentrating without having to try. It just happened. Saman knew general relativity tells us that what we call space is just another feature of the gravitational field of the universe. So space and space-time can and do not exist apart from the matter and energy that create the gravitational field. The universe is the totality of all space, time, matter, and energy.

The narrator went on: "Everything is energy, and everything connects to everything else. The water in the ocean and the clouds in the sky. The trees and animals. You, me, and the world around us. Everything comes from the same source and returns to it. Everything is one. Thoughts and feelings are energy as well, so everything we think and feel influences everything and everyone on this planet. In this way, we create our reality because mind rules over matter: without imagination, there is nothing."

Many things he now had did not exist before. Someone imagined it. The power of his thought sent waves of energy, positive energy, into time and space. The power of his imagination was so great that he created it out of matter, and it came into existence.

Saman had to use the power of his thought to figure out what he wanted to bring into existence. With focus, passion, and dedication, he would send positive energy waves out into time and space. His imagination would take form and shape if he acted on it.

The final piece is to get off his backside and do it. Napoleon Hill says the power of our thoughts can appropriate the infinite intelligence only by using it, and there must be faith backed by the definiteness of purpose. Then the subconscious mind, the gateway to infinite intelligence, takes over. Saman suddenly realized that the voice he heard told him to do what he had been doing all these years.

It was not the same as he had lamented. Before, he was using his talents to do other people's bidding. This time around, he would use the talents and skill he had honed in the last thirty-six years to do *his* bidding. He would do it his way, the way he had always lamented it should be to anyone who cared to listen to him. Then he had only told them what he thought needed doing, but he had not done it—not yet.

To succeed in creating that which he desired so passionately, he had only to *do* it. Now he was ready to *do* his bidding!

PART THREE

S aman knew that the challenge was to find the equilibrium between imagination, dream or vision, and reality—the point where dreams and reality meet.

Dreams and reality were both important to him and part of his life. Therefore, he understood why he kept moving between his dream world and reality. Just as an atom would vibrate about a point, so did he move between his imagination and reality.

In Saman's dream, the point where the water and the mist meet was a signal to him that both were part of his life. If he wanted to achieve something, he first had to imagine or dream it. When he could do that, he was ready to move into reality to create it.

The more precise he was about what he desired, the better he could harness the energy in the universe toward his desires.

"The energy in the universe connected everyone and everything," Saman tried to recall. "Moreover, energy can transfer from one object to another," he thought aloud. Saman remembered the physics experiment his teacher showed him in the laboratory. He had placed a marble on a flat ramp. He then rolled another marble toward it. When they collided, the stationary marble moved. He had witnessed the transfer of energy from one marble to another. Then it did not have any impact on Saman; it was just another experiment to remember when taking his physics tests.

Now Saman thought hard about the experiment. "If thoughts are energy, my thoughts can transfer energy to something else. I can also harness this energy from the universe. With an abundance of this energy, I will have increased the likelihood of creating what I desire." His excitement was growing; his eyes lit up, and he was thinking hard. Saman paid no attention to the passage of time. He was absorbed in his thoughts.

He began to understand the importance of appropriating the universal intelligence, which was energy, for his use. While energy could move or transfer from one object to another, it cannot evaporate into thin air and disappear. If he harnessed this energy but did nothing with it, it would flow to some other object or matter that attracted it.

Saman's definiteness of purpose should translate into a constancy of use in achieving that purpose. Then the harnessed energy would flow with it. The ongoing actions would harness more of it to complete the task when needed.

Saman had seen this before in his kitchen. When he heated the frying pan, it became hot, drawing heat energy from the fire. If he discontinued the heating, the pan would lose heat. If he kept it on the flame, it would continue to get hotter.

The key was to persevere even if he did not have a perfect plan. He had to work hard toward his goal, always having a definite image of what he wanted to create.

Saman now understood better how his thoughts impact the universe and draw universal intelligence to help him by doing what he had to.

It was so simple, yet why had he not realized it before? He was not focused; he was easily distracted. It was like in this nursery rhyme:

> Polly, put the kettle on,
> Polly, put the kettle on,
> Polly, put the kettle on,
> We'll all have tea.
> Sukey, take it off again,
> Sukey, take it off again,
> Sukey, take it off again,
> They've all gone away.

If you put the kettle on and then keep taking it off the stove, they would not have their tea, would they? He smiled as he thought about it.

Saman understood that before he embarked on his journey to creating a new life for himself—a life filled with success, happiness, and fulfillment—he must ensure that he would not quit.

What qualities and values do I need to realize my aspiration? he pondered. *Discipline.* His gut felt it. Saman took his notebook out and wrote it down.

Discipline

He knew it was one of his weaknesses. Strangely, this weakness emanated from his strength. His kindness and compassion were his big stumbling blocks.

Saman had told himself that he would make sure that he saved enough money to go on a holiday. He needed a break from all the hustle and bustle around him.

"I promise, we will go to Australia this June," Saman assured Jay. It was just after Saman had finished writing his first textbook, sacrificing the entire end-of-year vacation to help his team get the book out in time because the previous writers on the team had failed to meet the deadlines. Saman joined the team at the end of his full school year back in 1993 when the rest of the staff went off for their deserved break.

"Can you make the sacrifice for the sake of students in our schools? I know I am asking a lot from you, but we are desperate," the deputy director of the Curriculum Institute looked at Saman with hope in her eyes.

"Yes," Saman replied. He worked with the remaining two team members and got the book published just in time before the Approved Textbooks List went out to all the schools.

His deputy director called him to her office. She was not one to mess about with, but she appreciated what Saman had done. "You can have an extra week of holidays in June," she told him, and then she paused to study his reaction. There was none. "Did you hear what I said?" she continued. "You had given up the entire month of December."

Saman looked at her and smiled. "I understand." And then he turned and left the room. She watched him leave her office and nodded.

Saman, on the other hand, had written off the December vacation. He was, instead, delighted that he had an additional week in June to take Jay and his son to Australia.

Two weeks later, his sister-in-law approached Jay for a loan, as they had to move house rather unexpectedly. They had signed the option to purchase—OTP, for short—with the prospective buyer. However, they did not count on having to move out so soon. The buyer had sold his apartment to someone, and he was desperate to move into their apartment. He was within his rights to do so, but Jay's sister did not plan for it.

"We have set aside some money for the impending holiday in Australia. We can loan that money to your sister," Saman said to Jay, who was, of course, delighted to help. She still hoped Saman would take her on the holiday he had promised her. In the end, Jay was disappointed.

"Did someone not say that the successful man was one who did not give up even in the face of numerous setbacks?"

Saman paused as he was thinking about the second quality he needed.

"Perseverance," he wrote below *discipline.*

Discipline

Perseverance

Saman had lots of it. He had gone through many challenges in life, but he was not one to give in easily. That was just a characteristic he had inherited from his mother. Despite all the hardship, she just soldiered on, but she never let her children see her whenever she was feeling down. *Mom always wore a happy countenance. I must have got it from her.* Saman smiled to himself.

Next was hard work. Saman was not averse to working hard. Yet he was always thinking of working smart.

"What are our SMART goals?" his bosses always sang the same tune. So this was a mindset he had cultivated from his working experience. "Work SMART. Don't just work hard" was a refrain that rang out. Over the years, Saman had also helped his colleagues set specific, measurable, achievable, realistic, and time-bound goals and targets.

"There seems not much wrong with it," Saman tried to clarify the doubts he had about it. The main problem with it, though, was with the term *realistic.*

Every time Saman and his colleagues set their target, they would get queries if the target was realistic; and more often than not, they would end up moderating it to one that everyone felt was achievable.

It was this moderation that Saman felt stifled his energy and passion. He understood that setting moderate targets meant that they were more likely to meet them. If they set more challenging targets and failed to meet them, it was considered poor management.

Yet everyone told students in the same school where they were setting these targets to aim high. "Aim for the stars! If you miss them, you would still hit the moon."

The irony was lost on them but not on Saman.

"How could an organization that set moderate goals for itself stand in front of its young protégés and advise them the very opposite?" Saman reasoned with himself. "The vision is not aligned. Its values are not consistent," Saman would debate with himself. "No wonder the students and the organization seldom realize their true potential." It was different when Saman acted on his own.

"Do you know what the problem with that is?" Saman would tell his deputy. "We are boxed in by the structure or theory we adopt."

"What do you mean?" his deputy quizzed him. He was always open to new ways of perceiving things; Saman liked that because he reminded Saman of himself.

"Our SMART target tool says that if we have high expectations and we do not meet them, we will have to give ourselves a lower score. Setting a target of four hundred points and achieving 350 is considered poor management as opposed to setting a target of 250 and hitting three hundred, in which case, it's noted as having exceeded expectations."

"It's the self-fulfilling prophecy at work all over again. The structure we adopt drives our behavior, and so we set moderate targets to score better when, in reality, we could set higher targets and achieve more, although we may fall short of the target we set," the deputy reasoned.

"Exactly."

Saman wrote *hard work* followed by *high expectations*.

Discipline

Perseverance

Hard work

High expectations

He was doing his bidding this time. His vision aligned with his values. Saman felt he would not be at odds with his espoused theory and the theory in practice. It felt right.

To cultivate all these values—some of which he had in limited amounts, others which he lacked completely—Saman concluded, after much thought, that he had to work diligently on himself. He returned to the same realization he had had much earlier. He must look within himself. These were not qualities one could go and pick out from a shelf. No amount of money would buy them either. "Sadhguru says it requires inner engineering." Saman chuckled to himself; he liked the word *engineering*, used differently in this instance.

Ah yes! The Romans did not build their city in a day, Saman thought as he added the next value to his list.

Discipline

Perseverance

Hard work

High expectations

Patience

"I will not waver but show restraint in the face of any difficulty that may arise. I shall work hard, always striving to be the best I can be, and temper it by remaining grounded. I must celebrate any little success that comes my way, take baby steps toward my goal, and I will get there," Saman kept repeating to himself.

He focused on his list of words and decided that he would work on himself first. He rewrote his list of words as a to-do list:

To Do

Exercise self-discipline

Persevere to the end

Work hard

Set high expectations

Be patient

Saman studied his to-do list. He wrote it out in large print on a piece of white paper. Then Saman put it up on the bedroom wall facing him so that it would be the first thing he saw when he awoke each morning. He saw that it was good, and he was happy.

⟞⟞⦿⟝⟝

Life never failed to throw a spin ball every time Saman was enjoying himself. "Are you subtly trying to tell me that I need to change my attitude around here?" Jay glared at Saman as she looked at the bedroom wall and then at him.

"If truth be told, yes," Saman replied.

"What?"

Saman walked over to his wife, put his arm around her, and said, "These are reminders for me, Jay, but you are welcome to use them if you find they are relevant.

Jay frowned. *Is he needling me?* she thought to herself.

"I am not sending any hints to you. Seriously, they are for me to work on," Saman quickly replied, as he had become an expert at reading Jay's mind voice after thirty years of living under the same roof.

"Well, good luck then, but don't add to *my* to-do list of chores around the house, expecting me to clean the dust off the paper after some time," Jay rejoined.

"No, I won't."

Jay shot him her version of the incredulous look, which, by the way, Saman had also become accustomed to after thirty years. "You mean like the helping hand you and your two boys give me every day with the chores?" Then she smiled like the air stewardess would do in an advertisement, her closed mouth suddenly stretching out sideways and returning, almost immediately, to its original position.

Saman was now ready to start his new life. He resolved to take stock regularly by checking on his progress in cultivating the values he had put on his bedroom wall.

"Dad, are you serious about sticking to your plan?" his son asked him.

"Yes, of course. Why do you ask?"

"You have not kept to any of your new year resolutions so far," his son teased him.

"You're right about that."

"I have a suggestion, Dad."

Saman looked up from studying the WhatsApp message he had received from his anneh in KL: "Good morning," it read and continued: "When you deeply observe, everything is your teacher."

He looked intently at his son. "I'm listening," Saman replied.

"If you want to stick to your resolutions, why don't you get a small plant, something you like, and tend it every day?"

Saman did not understand what his son was driving at and cocked his head to one side, as he often did if he was not clear about anything.

His son recognized the signal. "Tending to the plant requires patience, and as you see it grow, you will feel committed to keeping to your resolutions. If it does not, it will tell you that you have not been nurturing enough toward it, just like your resolutions."

Saman looked at his son through new lenses; his boy had grown up. *He must have been observing me, and he knows my weakness.* "Sounds like a great idea, son. Will you help me pick up something from the plants' section at IKEA?"

"I'm afraid I can't do that, Dad."

"Why not?"

Saman's son shook his head in frustration. "You need to do it, Dad. It's part of the process. It's about your priorities, Dad," his son replied with mischief twinkling in his eyes.

Saman smiled at his son. He was throwing back Saman's words at him. Saman often told the boy to get his priorities right when he was still in school. Now that he was getting ready to do his National Service, Saman felt that his words had sunk in; if nothing else, his son had learned about priorities. Saman felt a sense of satisfaction combined with pride that his son was now his teacher.

"All right, all right, I'll get it. I'll do it myself, and I promise you that I will stick to my resolutions."

"Good," his son shot back. "I'll let you know how you are doing." And they both burst out laughing.

Saman looked at his bedroom wall again. He felt energized.

"What plant shall I get?" Saman wondered aloud after his son had left the room. "I need to make a trip to IKEA. I'll get Jay along for company. It's her favorite place. While she's busily engrossed in the furniture section, I'll have time to pick a plant. I'm going to be a gardener, a small one for a start," Saman told himself.

———————◆———————

Saman and Jay set off for IKEA, located at Queensway. Jay grew up in Queenstown, the first new town built in Singapore back in 1963. Her father bought a flat there for $6,200. It now sold for above $150,000. The Housing and Development Board was demolishing the blocks of apartments. Jay felt sad at the thought that they would soon be no more.

Saman and Jay took a bus to IKEA. They had to change several buses. As the bus passed Commonwealth MRT station, Jay felt nostalgic. Jay had not been back there since she got married. There was no reason to do so. Her whole family had moved out of the area after her sisters got married.

The bus then drove past the iconic Queensway Shopping Centre before it stopped slightly ahead of IKEA diagonally across from the shopping center. Jay recalled the trips there with her family. They did their Christmas shopping at Queensway Shopping Centre. She had heard that it was going to make way for new developments. Jay glanced back to take one last look at the building. Saman knew what she was thinking.

———————◆———————

"I'll be over at the furniture section," Jay called out to Saman, who was already heading toward where the plants and other gardening equipment were on display.

Saman turned to nod his acknowledgment. Jay noticed that he was unusually excited that day. *I hope he does not hurry me as he usually does*, Jay thought as a table lamp caught her attention. Soon she forgot about Saman.

"Can I help you, sir?" a voice interrupted Saman, who was looking at the little plants in even tinier flowerpots. Their quaintness drew him to them.

"You may," Saman replied. "I'm looking for a small potted plant that does not require too much attention."

"I'm afraid that plants need tender loving care, sir." The girl smiled at him. "The cacti may be what you want. They are quite hardy."

"Well," Saman hesitated, "I was hoping to get a flowering plant."

"Cacti do flower, sir." She handed him one from the lower shelf that she said had bright-pink flowers. Saman liked it.

"I'll take it." Saman beamed at the girl. She felt good. "You'll be able to advise me on how to care for it, won't you?"

"Yes, sir," she replied as she showed Saman a brochure that she took him through, explaining what he needed to do. "They do not require much water, though, but you have to sun them if you are keeping them indoors.

Saman intended to keep his cactus on the low cabinet just below the paper on his bedroom wall that reminded him of his resolution daily.

He thanked the salesgirl, paid for his purchase at the counter, and braced himself for the search that he was sure awaited him. He knew he would have a hard time looking for Jay, who usually found a way to get lost in the maze of furniture. *I think she might be in the decor section,* he thought and headed in that direction. Jay was there looking at tea lights. Jay loved the tea lights. She held four boxes, one in each color. Saman was pleased he had guessed right.

"Why are you smiling? I don't usually see that look on your face when we are at IKEA. Some salesgirl must have made your day." Jay wanted to divert his attention from the tea lights before he reminded her that there were still a few boxes of them at home. "But they are all white," she justified herself.

Saman's smile disappeared. Jay was right, though not quite, as the reason she had in mind was not exactly why he was smiling. "Look, I got a cactus plant, and it has flowers too."

Jay looked at what Saman was holding in his hands. "Where have the flowers gone?" she asked him.

"There aren't any flowers now, but after I look after them, they may start blooming anytime soon."

"They may," Jay replied and shrugged her shoulders. "I hope I don't end up having to look after them as well," she mumbled to herself as they left for home.

On the bus ride home, Jay kept glancing sideways at Saman, who was admiring his latest spindly acquisition. He told himself he would take them out for sunning every day lest they die.

"They don't usually die so easily," Jay interjected.

"What?"

"They are hardy plants. You do not need to water them every day, but—"

Before she could say any more, Saman cut in, "I will have to put them out in the sun."

"You have been reading up. But reading up alone will not do much for your cactus. You have to care for the plant." Jay rolled her eyes as she tried to get him to look at her.

"I know, Jay."

"It will do the cactus some good if you add fertilizers to it. Loosening the soil every once in a while helps as well. The only rule is, make sure the soil is dry between each watering. It will stop the roots and lower edges of the plant from rotting or becoming waterlogged."

Saman was impressed by her knowledge. She certainly seemed to know more than the salesgirl at IKEA. Jay had a minigarden in their home, and he knew that she knew a little about taking care of plants. He also felt confident because she was there. Despite the tone of her voice, Saman knew that she would be there to advise him.

———————◆———————

The first week, Saman excitedly watched his cactus to make sure it was growing well. Sometimes it was the first thing he looked at before reading his resolution on the wall.

When he was getting ready to water his cactus on the second week after he had brought it home, his son cautioned him, "Dad, don't give it too much water. It's a desert plant."

"Since when did you become such an expert on cacti?" Saman inquired.

"I am not, Dad."

"Then why this interest in my cactus?"

"Oh, it's nothing," his son replied as he returned his attention to the book he was reading.

Saman could sense that he was withholding something from him. He could see his eyes peering at Saman over the top of the book he was holding in his hands.

Saman stopped in his tracks and prodded his son for an answer, "What is it?"

"It's nothing. Mom just told me to make sure you do not water the cactus too often."

"So that's why you have been watching me like a hawk all morning," Saman declared triumphantly. "You and Mom do not trust me to look after my cactus."

His son laughed. "We do not want you to be disappointed if the plant, you know," he stopped.

"What? Dies?" Saman responded. "Let me tell you something, young man. I'll give the first flowers from my cactus to you and your mom." Saman watered his cactus then turned to his son. "Tell your mother that I last watered it a week ago. I need to water it weekly."

His son gave Saman the thumbs-up sign, but his dad was busy tending his cactus. The boy knew that his dad was going to succeed. Whenever he gave his full attention to something, he did.

<hr />

One could see the sense of satisfaction that glowed on Saman's face when he held up his cactus plant with its first bloom. There were tiny pink flowers that sprouted on the stem of the cactus plant. "Look." Saman held the plant toward Jay and his son, who were having their breakfast.

"What lovely flowers. You have done it, Dad," his son, who was his biggest benefactor in his endeavor to get his cactus to bloom, said.

"Not bad," echoed Jay.

Saman admired his cactus plant, and he turned it to examine it from every angle. He looked around to make sure no one was looking. Then he spoke to his cactus," I am proud of you. You look great when you are in full bloom." Then he looked toward the door to make sure that Jay wasn't looking. She was not.

Saman then studied the resolutions on the wall. "I have persevered because of my discipline and hard work tending my cactus plant every day. My patience has paid off. It has been worth my while waiting for it to bloom." Saman felt proud of himself. It had taken all of six months.

Cacti bear flowers about once a year, and the blooms can last up to six weeks—Saman found out from a book he borrowed from the Choa Chu Kang Library near his home. It was titled *The Complete Book of Cacti & Succulents*. The guidebook featured the history, cultivation, and imaginative use of more than three hundred succulents and cacti plants in comprehensive, easy-to-follow illustrated stages of their growth and development. The book offered in-depth information and lots of eye-catching photographs. Saman found everything he needed to grow his cactus into a healthy flowering plant.

"Dad?" his son interrupted his thoughts.

Saman shook out of his daydream and looked in the direction of the voice. He did not say anything.

"Surely you are not planning to become a full-time cactus farmer?"

Furrows appeared on Saman's forehead, as he did not understand what his son was getting at. Saman's eyes narrowed. His lips pouted, he gestured with his head at his son with a blank look on his face.

"I just want to remind you, lest you forget, that the cactus was merely to test your resolve."

"Test my resolve? At what?"

"At cultivating some of the values you need to embark on your big plan to start your life afresh, remember?"

The smug look on Saman's face gave way to a serious one. His eyes opened up a little as he nodded in agreement at his son. "I know," Saman replied. He was nearly distracted again from his goal. Yet he remembered that he had to celebrate every little success.

<hr />

It was the Christmas season again. There was much to do to spruce up the house as they did every year. Yet things did not seem to be moving as they should. Jay was always in a foul mood. "Nobody seems to be bothered to lift a finger to help me around the house."

Saman knew she was about to direct her frustration at him. He was right.

"The boys are all grown up now, but they do not help. You can tell them that they have responsibilities at home too."

"What is it that you want us to do? Why don't you come straight to the point?"

"The point I've been making is, I need you and the boys to help. It's only a week to Christmas, and the tree is not up. They want to have their friends over for Christmas, which means I have to prepare the dishes."

"So you are worried that the Christmas tree is not up yet? Is that it?"

Jay looked at Saman and stormed out of the living room. Saman darted out of the living room and went to the boys' room. "Listen, can you help to put up the Christmas tree?"

Saman's older son looked surprised. "Don't we do that every year?"

"Yes, but the issue is that it's not up yet, and your mother is on the warpath. Your brother is not pulling his weight as you do." Saman tried to play one boy against the other. It was his strategy.

"All right, Dad, let me handle this tonight."

Then Saman left the room. *One down,* he thought to himself.

When his second son returned from his gym workout, Saman spoke to him, "Look, I know you have just got your gym membership. It's a good thing, but you're out the whole time, and this is Christmas season."

"What about that, Dad?"

"Mom is on the warpath about how much work she has to do. She is complaining that nobody is helping her."

"What does she want us to do?"

"Nothing much. Mom wants us to put up the Christmas tree."

"That's it?"

"Yes. But your brother has classes, and he's not much help. He can help probably late in the evenings."

"Don't worry, Dad. Let me handle this."

Second one down, Saman thought to himself.

That afternoon, Saman's second son took out the Christmas tree from their storeroom, where it'd stay for a year every year, and he started setting it up. Saman was in the living room.

"The usual corner next to the sofa?" his son asked, pointing to the spot by the window. It was the space between the three-seater and the two-seater that were at right angles to each other.

"Yes, I guess so," Saman said, looking toward his bedroom to see if Jay might have any opinion. Jay walked past, glanced at her son setting up the tree, and walked on quietly.

"Silence means consent," Saman said to his son, who then worked quickly, and soon he had the three parts of the tree fixed, and it was standing tall again.

"What about the decor?"

"Your call," Saman replied.

"Are you sure, Dad? Please don't start by asking me to change after I have put all the decorations up."

Saman gestured with his thumb and forefinger that he had decided to keep his lips sealed, but his son did not look convinced.

Soon his older brother returned and offered to fix the two hundred white lights. He was good at electrical work. Soon the two boys had the tree lit up. They worked quietly. Then they took out the bag containing the decorations. They had many themes and color combinations accumulated over the years. The boys looked at each other, then the older boy asked, "What theme do you have in mind?"

Saman again gestured that it was up to the boys. Between them, they decided that they would go with the traditional red, silver, and gold color theme and set about putting up the shiny balls and reindeer. They fixed tinsels streamers and adjusted the decorations and the lights to make sure that the light shone on the decorations to get them to sparkle like stars.

Jay walked past the living room, and she glanced in the direction of the boys at work. She did not say anything.

So far, so good, thought Saman. He had managed to get the two boys to work together by snitching on one to the other. In the meantime, his wife was quiet.

Soon the Christmas tree stood tall again like a proud peacock preening itself with all the glory of its dazzling colors that glittered in the light. Saman felt that the two hundred minilights were obscuring the decorations, but he waited to see if Jay thought the same or otherwise. He would go along with her opinion if only to have some peace and happiness around the house. It was Christmas, after all. Saman wanted to use the opportunity to display the spirit of giving.

Finally, the boys waited for Jay to give their Christmas tree a once-over as she usually did every year, and they held out the star. Every year, Saman had the honor of placing the star.

"Dad, are you ready?" the two boys echoed together.

"I think it would be better if we get mommy to do it this year." Saman took the star and held it out to his wife.

Jay hesitated. "Why change?"

"Change is good, isn't it?" Saman replied. "I'd like you to do it this year."

"Go on then, Mommy," the two boys said.

Jay took the star, and she placed it on the top of the tree. Saman helped to fix it securely. Then they stepped back and looked at their Christmas tree. By that time, one of the boys switched on the lights again, while the other played Christmas carols on the new JBL portable speakers he bought as a Christmas present for Saman, but it was for everyone's enjoyment at home as well.

The Christmas tree glittered in the corner of their living room. The four of them looked pleased, and Jay was in a joyous mood. "I'll cut my Christmas pudding for you to try. It needs a bit more time to mature, but let's try it anyway." Jay made Christmas pudding every year, and she knew they all loved her pudding. Saman thanked his wife and his sons for their hard work. As for himself, he had exercised patience by not reacting to his wife's complaint earlier in the morning. He was succeeding slowly but surely. He knew that there was still much work for him to do, and he was ready.

———————————

The following day, the whole family decided to attend the weekday mass online. It was the week before Christmas, and they could not go to church because of the COVID-19 restrictions limiting attendance to the first fifty people who managed to book the slots.

Saman's older son, who was active in the church youth ministry, tried to book a slot to attend mass on Christmas Eve, but it was futile trying to do so when everyone else was doing the same thing. He could not get a slot for each of them. They usually attend the midnight mass when everyone would dress in their Christmas best. The church would be bursting at its seams as they sat shoulder to shoulder.

After Christmas mass, Saman's sons would invite their friends for wine, cakes, turkey, chapati (a flatbread made from wheat flour), and chicken curry. The star dish was, invariably, Jay's homemade pudding, which the boys' friends had come to relish over the years of Christmas Eve feasting at Saman's home.

Although they could not go to church on the eve, the usual gang insisted that it should not be an excuse to cancel the Christmas Eve party, and it was so.

During the online mass the family was following that morning on the week before Christmas, the Gospel reading, a passage from Matthew 7:21–29, drew Saman's attention as the priest read out the words: "Not all who say, Lord, Lord will enter the kingdom of heaven, but those who do the will of my father."

The words and the passage were not new, but the insight that Saman got that morning was. It suddenly occurred to Saman that the call was to do the father's will.

Saman reflected then that he had hardly noticed words and phrases like "Believe in me" or "Call my name"; instead it was "Follow me" and "Do my father's will." It was always a call to *action—to do*, not merely know or say or profess.

The online mass was over, and the rest of the family was getting ready for breakfast since they were all home that day. It was not often that they had the opportunity to eat together.

"Dad?" his sons called out to their father. Saman was still seated, staring at the screen. The video had ended; there was only a screenshot of the inside of the church. "The mass is over."

Saman came out of his hypnotic concentration, and he seemed to still be in deep thought. "Are you all right, dad?" His second son was puzzled because Saman was not a religious man, though he went along with the family to church and observed the rituals and traditions.

"Yes, I'm fine." Saman finally smiled. "Let's all eat, shall we?" he said to the still-confused family who was trying to work out what was on Saman's mind.

Later, Saman took out his notebook and scribbled inside it the insights and connections made in his mind. It was more regular now that he noticed a thread that seemed to connect these seemingly disparate philosophies.

The inspirational gurus had advocated the importance of taking action to achieve success. Saman made the connection for himself between that and what the priest had read. Going to heaven was the ultimate aim for the devoutly faithful, and it was clear that mere prayers and being present at mass, as Saman was that morning, were not going to help him get to heaven.

The recurrent message he was hearing was to act, to do. Saman was pleased. He had not done much, but he realized how to reach his goal. For the erudite Saman, he had to understand something well before he embarked on it, with some exceptions like when he succumbed to greed or folly.

Saman kept reminding himself that this insight and knowledge he had gleaned was not the end; it was the means. Saman had to put to use what he learned. Otherwise it would be as good as not having learned anything. He would be where he'd been all that while—stuck at the starting line.

———————— ◆ ————————

That night, Saman had a strange dream. He was walking through the streets of a foreign land with someone he seemed to know yet could not be sure who it was. His friend, an older woman, was following her acquaintance, who was a psychic.

Saman's friend beckoned him to follow her closely, as there were lots of people on the narrow street. They had to make their way by almost squeezing through between other people headed in the opposite direction. On both sides stood old brick buildings that looked like they were no less than a few hundred years old; their architecture was not one he had seen before.

Saman saw different road signs and a constant flow of old run-down cars among high-end luxury cars. He was amazed that sheer poverty stood side by side with extreme wealth. But the most astonishing part was the vibrations radiating from this strange and mysterious land.

Ana had most likely read his mind. Ana was the psychic whom Saman and his lady friend were following. As he was looking at the buildings along the street they were on, she said, turning to Saman, "Yes, everything here is full of mysticism, supernatural, and strange energies. The years under communism have not changed that. You are in Mother Russia, and religion, superstition, and magic have dwelled here since the dawn of time."

At sunset, they arrived in front of an old and unassuming building. Ana lived with her sister, also a psychic, in a small apartment. Their grandmother was a psychic too, and despite communist oppression, she had taught them the Orthodox faith and the practice of Russian magical arts.

As soon as Saman entered the apartment, his eyes were immediately drawn to a wall covered with icons and particularly drawn to one of them. The image drew him in like a magnet, so he put his luggage down on the floor and got closer. He felt as if angels were guiding him to this very holy relic. Saman did not have to say a word before Ana told him and his friend, "Yes, this is the Sacred Icon of Happiness."

Saman did not understand what she meant. His friend looked stunned. "This icon is like the holy grail for psychics all over the world, and it is the same for millions of other people too. It is a source of angelic and magical power, maybe the most powerful one there is," she said. Saman looked at the icon again with a new sense of wonderment.

"Indeed, there are many items all over the world that supposedly have great powers. This icon is one of them," Ana addressed Saman. "It is not the only one left of its kind. Popular belief has it that about eight people around the world own an Icon of Happiness." So one could imagine how astonished Saman was to be in the presence of one of them.

Then Ana set about explaining its history. Apparently, in 1703, Peter the Great decided to build his capital of Saint Petersburg. Hundreds of thousands of people lost their lives to perform that task. The authorities buried anyone who had died while building the city in a specific place near the city's border. Some monks then built a monastery on that place.

The first report about the powers of the Sacred Icon of Happiness could be traced back to 1715 in the writings of an Orthodox monk who wrote this: "On the mount of the martyrs, God has wept so that men could find joy and happiness. The brothers of the monastery are ceaselessly working to craft these holy images so that men might see the might of God achieved through miracles!" Ana explained. Ana continued to narrate the story of the Icon of Happiness. According to historical sources, monks crafted these icons in small numbers in that monastery very close to Saint Petersburg. Some writings mentioned processions and pilgrimages happening once every seven years, and someone in the crowd would receive the icon. The person selected to receive the icon would immediately find themselves full of luck and prosperity!

During the 1917 revolution, almost all these holy images got destroyed. And for seventy years, the communist regime tried to snuff out any belief or religion and psychic abilities, but their efforts were in vain. Former monks kept fashioning the magical icons through cloak-and-dagger means. Anna told them some people were saved from Stalinist purges and deportations because they worked on this icon. Her eyes became moist as she looked away at the small window at the top of the apartment. A ray of light from the streetlights outside shone through.

Then Ana's sister joined in. She explained that presently, according to popular belief, there were still Fathers who handcrafted the Sacred Icon of Happiness. But it had been impossible to make contact with one of these Fathers for many years. However, one thing was indisputable: the small monastery was still standing.

"Now that you know the story behind this icon, you must be wondering why the Icon of Happiness is known to perform miracles." Ana asked them. Both Saman and his friend nodded. "For now, here is what experts are saying about the mysterious power of this icon: Firstly, they crafted the icon at the monastery of the martyrs. Thousands of people died, and God took pity on their souls. It became a holy place. In other words, one can feel the presence of God in this location. Anything crafted there by people devoted to God becomes *magical*. Secondly, the holy image itself. Monks have been using the same handcrafted illumination techniques for generations. Today we know that shapes and colors have a direct influence on the aura and phenomena related to luck," Ana explained.

"These are the only rational explanation for the powers of the icon. Do you need to be a practicing Orthodox to benefit from its magic power? You don't. The icon is a holy item, the light of God in a way, and God does not mind your color or religion or whether you are a practicing believer or not. God only looks inside the hearts of people. That's all." Ana then looked directly into Saman's eyes.

Ana's sister then said to Saman, "The celestial powers chose you to receive this icon on the day you were born. It has taken all these years for you to arrive here."

Then a door opened in the wall of the apartment, and Saman followed Ana in. His friend waited outside. It was a small cloister. In the dancing light of the candles and the thick incense smoke, Saman could make out the figure of a man. An old Orthodox priest was standing before an altar.

Ana motioned Saman to wait for her. She went to see the man before waving Saman to her. She introduced him to Father Victor. Acting as an interpreter, Ana explained that Father Victor and other Brothers of the Order continued the ancestral work of crafting one holy icon each year.

They spoke for a long while, and the brother decided to entrust Saman with an icon, just one, under the following conditions: People who could receive this icon must have a pure heart, regardless of their belief in any specific God or faith, as long as they'd strive to do good and refrain from harming others. They must also be full of discretion, especially around money, and make sure that they wouldn't draw attention to themselves. These people must vow never to invoke the icon to fulfill any desire that broke any divine law. Finally, at least once a month, these people must recite the prayers of happiness bestowed on the monastery, a legacy shared from each generation to the next.

Father Victor handed Saman the icon. He then asked him for a donation for the brothers of the monastery.

Ana explained a belief held in Russia: a donation should match the worth of anything you'd receive as a gift. So Saman removed a chain he was wearing, which was worth a lot of money, and made his donation.

Ana explained that her people were happy to share whatever they had even when they didn't have much. "It comes from their heart. And it also comes from my heart when I want to share this great secret of happiness with you."

Saman awoke with a start. The phone on the side table beside him showed it was three thirty-three in the morning. He turned to his right and saw Jay fast asleep. Her snore was reverberating around the room. *What a strange dream. What did it all mean?* Saman was still in disbelief. As was his usual practice when his sleep was interrupted, he got out of bed to fetch a glass of water, which he promptly downed. Then he got back into bed. He kept thinking about the promise of happiness that the owner of the icon would experience. As Saman thought about it, he realized that every endeavor anyone undertook was, ultimately, in pursuit of happiness, which, incidentally, is attained by becoming a self-fulfilled person. He soon dozed off again with that thought in mind.

———————•◆•———————

A newfound vigor woke Saman up. He looked at his bedroom wall. The icon he expected to see was not there. Saman searched the pockets of his shorts, but nothing there either. Then he started to remember his strange dream in bits and parts. He certainly had remembered an icon that he received. He remembered also that it brought happiness to anyone who owned it. It suddenly dawned on him that the means to that happiness was by seeking self-actualization. That was the last thought on his mind before he slept off. Saman remembered that clearly.

The icon was a symbol; it stood for happiness. All that one pursues—wealth, health, love, family, friends, success in business or work, knowledge, peace of mind, safety, anything desirable that one desires—was to experience happiness.

Yet his inner voice told him that many people had these things but were still not happy. "Why?" Saman asked himself.

Saman felt it was because, internally, they were not happy with what they had. "I must learn to be happy inside me. All that I pursue can make me happy, but I must choose to be happy. In themselves, all these external pursuits do nothing. It is my response to them that does something to me. Happiness comes from inside me."

Saman told himself that he would try to be happy with what he had achieved at the end of each day. If he maintained this state of mind, he would not only continue being happy but also the happiness within him would grow.

Saman then declared aloud, "That is it! Self-actualization." Saman sprang out of bed. He found his icon of happiness. Now he had to work to first be happy by choice. Then he'd work harder to be happier still by design.

———————◆———————

Saman took out his sacred notebook, his guide to happiness.

"My strategies to realize happiness," Saman wrote on a new page. He looked at it. It looked good:

My strategies to realize happiness

Saman thought hard to recall all that he had learned and digested. He wanted to access only that which he had connected when he saw the links between them. He would leave out the rest of the clutter.

Faith came first, then purpose and plan. Next, Saman put down "clear visualization of the end." Saman smiled to himself as he gently knocked his head with his knuckles. "Action, stupid." Saman then reworded his strategy in actionable terms:

My Strategies for Success

Begin by having unwavering faith
Write down my purpose clearly
Work out my plan with details
Visualize my success
Put it up on the wall

Saman looked at his notes, and he was happy. He told himself that he would take baby steps. Having started by writing down his strategy, it was cause for celebration. It was his choice to be happy.

Walking up to his cactus plant, Saman spoke to it. "Thank you. You have inspired me to persevere and to have patience. I want to feel the joy I felt when you first bloomed. I shall work on my strategies, and you will reward me with the next bloom of your pink flowers. I shall wait even if it takes six months." Saman then pushed his fist toward his cactus plant. It would be their secret deal.

"What are you doing being up so early in the morning?" Jay asked Saman. "It's only five."

"It's my first day at work, Jay."

"What do you mean? You are retired and have been for the past year," Jay replied, looking at Saman with her half-open eyes. She was a little worried Saman had lost his mind. "It's okay, dear, get back to bed." And she tossed the blanket over herself.

Saman smiled back at his wife. He was often amazed at how quickly she could fall asleep. He had read that it was people who had no worries in their life who slept like that. "Well, at least she is happy," he mumbled to himself.

Within fifteen minutes, Saman had got ready and was doing the five exercises recommended by the *The Elixir of Life* book that he had been reading. The five moves gave him the youthful vigor that he had before. They were yoga moves combined with isometric exercises that involved stretching. His chakras would realign and start spinning like they do in youth.

Saman's first exercise was to stand with his feet slightly apart and his hands held out at shoulder height. Then he started to spin in a clockwise direction. But he kept his focus on a fixed point on the wall each time he completed one spin. That ensured he would not lose his balance.

Saman picked the family photo taken in Melbourne in 2017 when they visited there as a reward for his second son after he had done well in his examinations. Saman picked it deliberately to remind himself that by keeping up with his exercise routine, he would get his reward too. Saman had decided that keeping faith in his journey toward his goal would begin with a healthy body and mind.

After his workout, Saman took a quick shower and did his daily prayers that took the better part of the next hour. It was sevenish when he sat down at his laptop to begin writing.

Saman had written several nonfiction books before as he worked with the Curriculum Institute. He aspired to become a writer of fiction.

Saman's purpose was to bring together all his life experiences and to share them with others. Then they would make fewer mistakes as they embarked on their life journey. Saman knew that there was no shortcut to this learning journey.

Yet Saman had learned from other experts in their field of work and their life experiences. By sharing what he knew, Saman was self-actualizing as well. He felt his purpose in life was to help others by shining a light through the fog of confusion that characterized the world they lived in so that they could see a little better. Saman remembered the words on the first page of *Principia Mathematica* by Sir Isaac Newton:

> If I have been able to see further, it has been
> by standing on the shoulders of Giants.

What a humbling thought from one of the greatest scientists who ever lived, Saman thought to himself. *Every man learns from everyone else who came before him. We can go further because of the lessons we learn from others who came before us. It connects everyone to everyone else. Having been able to see a little further, don't we owe it to those who come after us to shine the light for them to look ahead?*

His purpose was clear. He wanted to share his experience for the benefit of his children and his children's children. He would use his talent and his love for words to do that. That would also keep him going. Saman would be doing his bidding.

***

Jay was surprised to find Saman engrossed at his laptop. "Would you like a cup of coffee?" she asked just to make sure he was feeling fine.

"Uh-uh," he snorted. He had had his cupper, which he must have every morning.

"Toast with half-boiled eggs?" Jay knew they were his idea of a good breakfast. Saman had often shared with his wife that, growing up in Kluang, he and his cousins looked forward to toast and eggs in the morning.

Uncle Louis, a technician at the nearby Telecommunication Department, would complete taking the roster with his gang of laborers then assign them their first tasks for the morning by seven thirty and then head back home for breakfast. Work officially started at nine.

Uncle Louis's daily breakfast regime was two slices of toast, lightly buttered, and two half-boiled eggs. Aunt Louisa toasted the bread over a firewood stove. They had a wire-mesh homemade toaster. She would put the bread between the two flaps of the toaster, which was then held over the red-hot cinders, not the fire. Toasting the bread when the fire was still burning would char it. But done over hot coals would toast it evenly on both sides while flipping the toaster over every few minutes.

Every day, Uncle Louis would give a mouthful of buttered toast slathered in the half-boiled egg to one of the younger children. Saman and his younger cousins looked forward to their turn. The toast and eggs tasted extra special when Uncle Louis fed it to them. It was Uncle Louis's way of showing his love to them. The happy child would run off to fetch the morning papers to Uncle Louis, who would browse through the day's news before he reported back to work.

The offer of his favorite breakfast by Jay did not distract Saman. Not able to take it any longer, Jay walked up behind her husband to steal a peek at what had kept him glued to the screen of his laptop. Saman was typing furiously. Jay smiled and tiptoed to her morning chores, which were waiting for her. She usually put the clothes into the washing machine, swept the house if she had time before taking her shower, and head off to school, where she taught little toddlers. Jay was an early-years teacher. She, too, passed on her learning after she struggled through the early years of parenting her two boys to the toddlers under her care.

Saman was still at his laptop when Jay returned home in the evening. "Have you taken your lunch? Did you stop to eat something? It's not good to sit all day without stretching your limbs and relaxing your eyes, you know?" She was echoing the same things she says to her children at school every day.

Saman looked up as he was finishing the last paragraph of his first chapter. "Yes, thank you, I did." He then completed what he was writing, took a look at his work, and smiled. Saman had written ten pages on the first day. He would have to edit his writing later and redraft parts that he wanted to improve.

But first, he needed a glass of water. Somehow all that work at the keyboard made him thirsty as if he had been laboring under the sun. Beads of sweat clung to his eyebrow. They looked as if they were perched at the edge of a waterfall, ready to fall any moment now. Saman felt liberated as his spirits soared after he had taken his first sojourn toward his goal. He was pleased.

Saman had contacted a local publisher he knew from his years of working on school textbooks.

"Why don't you send me a copy of your first chapter? Let me take a look and come back to you in a week. Is that all right?"

"Yes, of course. Thank you. I'll send it to you right away."

Saman had been working on his book every day. He planned to write for three hours each day—two hours in the morning when it was quiet, and then he would write for an hour in the evening. At night, he polished what he had written. Sometimes he worked through the late hours of the night until he was satisfied.

Surprisingly, Saman did not feel tired or exhausted. Often when he had completed his redrafting, he felt a surge of energy within him. Doing what you love would do that, Saman realized. He often went to bed happy.

<hr />

The mobile phone on the side table in the bedroom buzzed continuously. Jay picked it up. It was an unknown number.

"Hello?" The voice on the other side sounded excited. "Saman?"

"Hello, Saman's in the shower. Who is this, please? Is anything the matter? Can I get him to call back?"

"It's all right. Please tell Saman to call me back at this number as soon as he can, thank you."

When Saman got out of the shower, Jay told him. "Why did you not tell me?" Saman said when he looked at the number of the caller. Saman got dressed quickly and dialed the last number on his phone. The phone was engaged. He called again, and after two more attempts, someone answered his call.

"Is that Saman?"

"Yes!" Saman was anxious.

"Hang on awhile, Saman." Someone had interrupted the caller. Saman overheard their conversation.

"If he can come down this afternoon with his manuscript, I should be in the office. I'm flying out tomorrow. You know, with this travel bubble they have between Singapore and Hong Kong, if I miss this flight, I will have to wait a couple of weeks to catch the next one. Head office will not be pleased. I will be back only after a fortnight," the other voice said, sounding a little agitated.

"Yes, of course. I'll get the message across that it's urgent."

"Hello? Saman? Look, I have an urgent meeting in a few minutes. Would you be able to swing by my office this afternoon at ten past two?"

"Ten past two? Sure."

"You know where it is. You've been here before."

"Yes. Yes, I do."

"Bring along whatever you have written even if it is not complete. The editor in chief wants to take a look. He has seen the chapter you sent to me. It's urgent, as he'll be out of town for two weeks after today."

Saman was excited to receive the news. He was not sure what the meeting was going to be about exactly, but he had heard enough over the phone to guess hopefully. He had to seize the opportunity when it presented itself.

It was nine thirty. Saman still had four hours and forty minutes to go. He distracted himself from doing too much thinking by busying himself with getting all his things ready in his bag. He stuffed his laptop into the bag as well and his thumb drive.

Jay had already left for work. She was late for work; her shift started at nine that day. Jay and her coteachers took turns to work on staggered starting times from seven in the morning to seven in the evening when the parents came to fetch their children home. They each did eight-hour shifts, starting thirty minutes after their colleague.

Saman sat on the sofa by the window. He was alone with his thoughts. He remembered visualizing the completion of his work each night before he went to bed. Saman saw himself working feverishly at his laptop. He then saw his book taking shape, and soon he had completed it. He spoke to a local publisher who arranged for him to meet with his superiors. They looked pleased and made Saman several offers, of which he picked one. Then they signed on a document, and Saman shook hands with the publishers.

Fast-forward, and Saman saw his books on the shelves at the local bookstores. He saw himself browsing through the books at the Popular Bookstore at the shopping mall near his home. Saman also saw his books on the shelves at Kinokuniya, a well-known bookstore that carried the best writers' works. He saw his name clearly on the books on display at the "latest books" section: Saman L.

It started drizzling, and Saman got up to pull the windows in so that the rainwater would not come in. When Saman turned to leave, something caught his attention. Saman noticed his cactus on the windowsill. It seemed to be calling out to him to pick it up. He hadn't spoken to it in a while, although he did not forget to water it and check on it. Saman was busy trying to finish his book. There was nothing unusual about his cactus. He felt the urge to pick it up to say sorry.

Saman picked up his cactus from the windowsill and inspected it. He turned it around to look at it from every angle as he usually did. *There shouldn't be anything different,* he thought to himself. *I watered it only yesterday.* But his cactus plant was in bloom again. There were tiny pink buds on the stem. He did not notice them at first because they were on the side facing the outside.

Saman smiled at his cactus. "Thank you. I know you will reward me for my patience and hard work," Saman told his cactus. "Did you decide to reward me for tending to you every day without fail?" Saman knew that he had stuck to his resolution and focused on his cactus. The reward came unexpectedly when he least expected it.

Saman had not noticed the passing of time. It was half-past one. When he was in the company of his cactus, time was not on his mind. Saman got up to leave for his meeting. Just then, he had a thought. He went into his bedroom to look at the wall facing his bed one more time. There it was in all its simplicity, nothing pretentious. If not for its reminder every morning, Saman knew he would not have reached today. He recalled his recurrent dream where he wavered at the edge where the water and mist of cloud met. This time he had made his choice. This time he had dared. And he was ready to soar. He heard the cheers in the distant background.

Saman had set his mind on realizing his goal, and he worked hard until he got there. He had discovered the secret path to success; this would be the only path. Saman then read the words on the two pieces of paper again. It was in his handwriting.

To Do

Exercise self-discipline
Persevere to the end
Work hard
Set high expectations
Be patient

My Strategies for Success

Begin by having unwavering faith
Write down my purpose clearly
Work out my plan with details
Visualize my success
Put it up on the wall

EPILOGUE

Saman arrived at the office on the dot; it was five past two. The office staff was returning from lunch.

"Saman, you're here," the publisher who had spoken to him said as he looked at his watch. "And you are just in time for the meeting with the editor in chief."

"Good afternoon," said a nervous-looking Saman, and he held out a large envelope containing the manuscript of his book. "They are all in here—all 158 pages." They both smiled at each other as the other man accepted the envelope and showed Saman into the conference room for the meeting that would take place in two minutes.

The editor in chief, a scruffy-looking man, appeared from another door adjoining the conference room. Saman surmised that the door must be the entrance to the chief editor's room. As if reading Saman's thoughts, the man said, "I just came from my office," and he held the door open. Saman could see piles and piles of paper on the desk. There were more stacks of envelopes and books all around the desk, on the floor.

"Pardon the untidiness, but I know where my things are," he said, looking at Saman with an air of assuredness.

"Oh, that's all right," Saman replied. But his mind was all on what the man was going to say to him. He did not have to wait long.

"Look, Saman, I'll cut to the chase. I've looked at your first chapter, and I like it as well as the prologue. I can see that you've given it much thought, and I can't wait to read the rest of the manuscript. But John here will go through them first." He pointed at the publisher, who nodded in acknowledgment.

Saman could tell that John had a lot of respect for the editor in chief, as he stood there listening attentively, his hands held firmly by his sides like a schoolboy reporting to his teacher.

The editor in chief stood up and walked around his desk toward Saman. He held out his big burly hands, grasped Saman's right hand, and shook it as he gave Saman a look that told him he had lots of appreciation for his work. "We are glad to publish your book, but we will need to finalize our offer after looking at the rest of the manuscript. We are making you a tentative offer, you understand?" he said as he looked at Saman and then at John.

"I'll explain the terms and conditions to him, sir."

"And you will have to sign the exclusive rights clause," the man in charge said, looking at Saman. "John will explain the implications of that. Now if you will excuse me, gentlemen, I've got a flight to catch in two hours. Good luck and welcome on board." He nodded at Saman and walked back through the door he had come out of earlier.

Saman did not remember anything the editor in chief had said to him after he had said, "We are glad to publish your book." Those were the words he wanted to hear, and that was all he heard.

His friend, the publisher, shook hands with Saman and was saying something to him. But Saman was so overcome with pride and joy that he just smiled and kept nodding at everything. Finally, he managed to express his thanks.

Then Saman called his son. "I did it!"

"Dad?" the voice on the other side replied.

They both fell silent after that for a long while. The same emotion welled up in both Saman and his son. No more words needed to be said.

ACKNOWLEDGMENT

I have quoted and paraphrased the great teachers such as Buddha, Jesus, Leonardo da Vinci, Samuel Coleridge, Lord Alfred Tennyson; other inspirational leaders like Carl Jung, Napoleon Hill, Sadhguru, Warren Buffet, John Lennon, Norman Schwarzkopf; and scientists such as Sir Isaac Newton and Albert Einstein.

As a student of life and lifelong learning, I am deeply indebted to them, my parents, and my teachers for enlightening me on my journey through life.

CPSIA information can be obtained
at www.ICGtesting.com
Printed in the USA
LVHW051640240523
747950LV00001B/2